# ABOUT T(

Aidy's just punched a co-worker, but he hasn't got time to deal with the fallout. With a deadline fast looming, he must get home, knuckle down and finish the story he's been working on, a story he hasn't been able to stop thinking about. It's the story of a falling plane and of a grieving mother.

Set across seventy-two hours, *About to Fall Apart* is the exhilarating story of a man of mixed heritage – given up for adoption as a kid and living on the Irish border – desperately trying to stay positive, to connect with his children and maybe even to find his own birth mother before it's too late.

09.04.2026

HB | 9780571392681 | £12.99
Ebook | 9780571392704
Audio | 9780571392711

For publicity enquiries please contact
josh.smith@faber.co.uk

Ashley Hickson-Lovence was born in London in 1991 and is a former secondary school English teacher. He earned his PhD in Creative and Critical Writing at the University of East Anglia. He has lectured English and Creative Writing at Brunel University, Arts University Bournemouth, University of East Anglia and the University of Suffolk. He is the author of the poetry collection *Why I Am Not a Bus Driver*, the acclaimed novels *The 392* and *Your Show*, and the 2024 prize-winning YA novel in verse *Wild East*.

*by the same author*

**THE 392**
**YOUR SHOW**
**WILD EAST**
**WHY I AM NOT A BUS DRIVER**

# ABOUT TO
# FALL APART

## ASHLEY
## HICKSON-LOVENCE

faber

First published in 2026
by Faber & Faber Limited
The Bindery, 51 Hatton Garden
London EC1N 8HN

Typeset by Faber & Faber Limited
Printed and bound by CPI Group (UK) Ltd, Croydon, CRO 4YY

Extract from 'Unholy Sonnet 9'
reproduced with permission © Mark Jarman

*This is a work of fiction. All of the characters, organisations and
events portrayed in this novel are either products of the author's
imagination or are used fictitiously*

A CIP record for this book
is available from the British Library

ISBN 978–0–571–39268–1

Our authorised representative in the EU for product safety is
Easy Access System Europe, Mustamäe tee 50, 10621 Tallinn, Estonia
gpsr.requests@easproject.com

2 4 6 8 10 9 7 5 3 1

For Dad. RIP.

Someone is always praying as the plane
Breaks up, and smoke and cold and darkness blow
Into the cabin. Praying as it happens,
Praying before it happens that it won't.

'Unholy Sonnet 9' by Mark Jarman

# FRIDAY

A IDY DIDN'T WANNA PUNCH HIM / HE REALLY DIDN'T
/ but that guy had it coming / & now the knuckles
of his right hand are throbbing / bulging baby-
cheek pink / he's gritted-teeth seething / speeding
out of the car park gripping the steering wheel
of his Qashqai handlebar-tight / his fist stings /
blood seeping sore / slow gushing burgundy / red
to darker red / he's been taunted since a toothless
toddler / called all sorts / but even now / after all
these years / it's hard not to retaliate when people /
colleagues / friends even / can't see past the darker
tinge of his skin / he's heard every slur imaginable
/ but *that* word in particular still arouses a fury in
him impossible to ignore / impossible to control
sometimes / he's red-face enraged / fury pulsing all
through his body skidding into the Spar / charging
through the forecourt / marching inside not to

pay for petrol but two six-packs / crisps & cans /
doesn't bother with a plastic bag / in his own half-
arsed way / you could say / he's doing his bit for
the environment / it's not what the scientists spout
that scares him / or how hot the planet will get in
a decade or two / he'll be long dead before then /
definitely doesn't listen to those poxy politicians /
but there's something Aidy finds oddly unnerving
about that Greta Thunberg / like he's being scolded
for his laissez-faire attitude to the so-called climate
. . . crisis? / emergency? / catastrophe? / whatever
it's being called these days / personally / he fumbles
with his purchases as he digs into his back pockets
for his car keys / cradling the cold cans of stout
close to his chest / stumbling back to his car /
manages to bleep it open with a spare finger / hops
in / dumps the goods in the cold passenger seat &
breathes long & hard / in & out / in & out / in &
out / he's so furiously thirsty he's tempted to crack
open a can now / right here by the petrol pumps
/ but as he stretches over to pick one up he stops
/ hesitates / decides to wait / can't take the risk of

potentially getting himself into more trouble after
what's already happened this afternoon / switches
the engine back on instead / puts his foot down /
pulls back out onto the main road leading towards
Belleek / traffic lights staying green / shuttling
on quickly along Boa Island Road / a red-knuckle
ride towards the border / sneaks a peak of Lough
Erne / uses the view to quell some of the fire inside
/ straddles it sometimes further downstream for
early-morning weekend walks / seeking a much-
needed respite from the weight of the week gone /
& the heavy load of the one to come / but today /
right now / he's going much too quick to properly
take it in / & with every inch he gets further away
from the scene of this latest misdemeanour / the
closer he gets to home & the start of the weekend
that could change his life / he feels gradually calmer
/ little by little / up ahead he sees a blonde jogger
skipping along the side of the road / donning bright
neon sportswear / tights but no shorts / vest / legs
/ bare arms / white Nike socks pulled all the way
up / as he drives past / craning his neck to have a

good look / sees she's all limbs & muscle / making her long run for the week look easy / effortless / on another day he might be inspired to stretch his legs a bit himself / got his treadmill in the garage / but for now / it's not in this weekend's itinerary / he's in a hurry / there's something important to do / somewhere more important to be / he speeds up by easing down on the accelerator pedal / temporarily shrugs off an ever-growing fear / an ever-increasing anxiety of going too fast / watches the needle rise / spike left to right / imagines head-on impact / oncoming cars spun out of control / debris strewn across the road / headlights in the hedge / newspaper headlines / funerals / coroner's reports / & then / before it gets too much / much too real / suddenly snaps himself out of it again / he needs to save this imagination for when he's sat in front of his laptop / needs to save this level of intensity for later / he imagines the lines spilling out of him like he's Ireland's answer to Stephen King / while sitting at his dining room table / the tips of fingers red / raw / sore / wrists stiff / cursor dancing across the

screen / too *in the flow* to falter / too *in the zone* to
slow / too *in the mood* to stop / using the pain from
his knuckles / numbing now a little thankfully /
to push on / it's a wound that will have to be dealt
with on Monday / Aidy knows / as the bleeding
stops & the scabbing starts / but he'll worry about
the possible repercussions later / it's a few minutes
before five when Aidy speeds into his drive / parks
up all askew / hops out with the urgency of needing
a piss but his bladder is far from full / right now
he has to get in quick / get his laptop open / he has
lines to write / a tale to tell / for a short story prize
/ the deadline is Sunday night at nine / 'up to five
thousand words' the guidelines said / the winner
gets a chance to work with a real editor / a copper-
bottomed guarantee to receive proper feedback on a
work-in-progress / free tickets / & accommodation
/ to West Cork Literary Festival down in Bantry
this summer / it's everything Aidy needs right now
/ after years of trying to make something of himself
as a poet of sorts / penning odes about ageing /
sonnets about dying / little limericks about the ups

& downs of life / scouring creative writing groups
on Facebook to join / a community he could be a
part of / signing up for last-minute open-mic slots
in half-full pubs / spending most of his savings self-
publishing a thousand copies of his poetry pamphlet
during the pandemic / boxes of them still sitting
in the garage / next to the treadmill / still nothing
meaningful has come of it / so he changed tack /
started working on something bigger a few years
ago / but after countless queries to literary agents
across the island of Ireland / England / the world /
only a handful bothered replying / the best he has
got so far for all those hours / days / weeks / months
/ years / decades / of note-scribbling & scalp-
scratching / all that effort he's put in / has been a
single / yes just one / personalised email response:

Many thanks for submitting. In spite of its qualities,
I'm not 100 per cent best placed for this and am
afraid I don't have the capacity to take it on currently.
Wishing you the best success . . .

. . . but this is the first time in a while / at least over
a year / that he has an idea he's genuinely excited
about / hopeful about even / an idea that he's been
thinking about for months / an idea he's let grow
& bloom while he thought it through & now feels
ready to use this furious fire burning big in his belly
to set it free / finally / & trust me / it has taken
courage to take the plunge / show up & start / two
finger type the first few lines / but the timing feels
right to give it a proper go / he might not have a job
come Monday morning / & probably won't look for
a new one either / not now at his age

/ / /

inside instantly feels much cooler than outside / he
eyes the thermostat / ponders switching the heating
on / does the sums / tots up the numbers / counts
up to a figure using his good hand / then decides
against it / doing this place up has cost a small
fortune already / & everything is too expensive
these days as it is / he's not keen to spend any more

than he has to / still got the back of the garden to
finish & the garage to sort out / he thumbs the
buttons of his Bluetooth speaker / shuffles 'Calming
Classical' on Spotify / lets the opening notes of
Debussy enter the space before scurrying back to
his car to get the crisps & drinks he bought / inside
/ in the little cluttered kitchen / the refrigerator
hums / a polka-dotted mug that says **TEA TIME IN
DONEGAL** rests on a threadbare dishcloth / in
between the little kitchen & the living room / in a
little nook / the screen of the CCTV live feed
flickers & ticks / flickers & ticks / Debussy blaring
loud now as Aidy re-enters seconds later / one of
the cans slowly slipping from under his forearm /
but he makes it / just / to the kitchen counter
before the can cannons to the ground / with eager
hands & a rumbling tummy Aidy rips open his first
packet of cheese & onion Taytos / stuffs in as many
as he can / they don't all make it into his mouth
first time / crumbs rain down his shirt / down to his
belly / one whole one on the floor / bends down /
eats it / faithful five-second-rule believer / flips

laptop open / types in his password extravagantly
like he's a pianist / proper over-the-top / feels like
Beethoven / or Jamie Cullum / clicks open his
project-in-progress / Microsoft Word / not high-
tech enough for Google Docs yet / starts reading
what he has so far from the top / but something's
wrong / words all fuzzy / not coming through clear
/ glasses / Aidy needs his glasses / he gets up /
retrieves them from his jacket pocket & returns to
his office chair with the padded armrests ready to
get to work / it doesn't take long to read what he
has already / just two lines / not even a title yet /
but he's got to start somewhere / so with a deep
intake of breath he writes a line / then another one
/ then one after that / then another one still /
before long he has written half a page / he adds a
comma / takes away a comma / splits a long
paragraph into two / fuses them together again / &
then after a sip of his Guinness which has now
settled delicious in his Man United pint glass / splits
them up again / gets to the end of a sentence /
breathes in / feels as light as an empty crisp packet

blowing in the wind / then breathes out / adding &
tweaking things as he scrolls down / eats more
crisps / lets them fizz on his tongue like communion
wafers / this is good / he thinks / a solid start / fear
of the blank page gone / you can't edit words that
aren't there & in less than hour he's making decent
progress / nowhere near what he needs yet / but
something to fiddle with later / tamper about with /
touch up & tweak / fine-tune & finesse / sips more
of his drink / pleased / goes for a piss / that
hedgehog is back / has made Aidy's garden his
home of late / slowly shuffling in the grass /
sniffing & snuffling in the undergrowth looking for
worms / feels safe enough not to hide / moments
later Aidy returns without washing his hands / fuck
it / he thinks / it's Friday / rules out the window /
& anyway / no time to waste / he has a deadline to
meet / he gets back to work / his main character / a
professional footballer at the peak of his career / has
now arrived at the airport / despite some earlier
trepidation / nervousness of the unknown / he's
here on the terminal concourse & he knows it's

time to kick on / sharpen up / pull up his socks &
stand up tall / show the world he's ready / ready to
prove himself on the biggest stage / ready to give it
his all for his new team / ready to start a new life at
a new club / further his career / make a name for
himself in the biggest & best league in the world /
training starts tomorrow afternoon & he's keen to
make a good first impression / Aidy captures it all /
word by word / line by line / tries to anyway / as
his now anxious protagonist goes through passport
control / & then security / heads to the gate / he's
dead tired / flat-out exhausted / it's been a mad few
days but he's made it / he's here / on the runway in
one piece / but then / as he spots a little old plane in
the distance across the tarmac / his stomach has a
sudden funny turn / flips 360 / he really hopes this
shabby thing isn't meant for him / it's tiny / old too
/ not at all state-of-the-art / far from pristine / just
a small-looking six-seater / parked in the corner
like the last to get picked for a game of playground
footy / but despite his unease / it's too late to turn
back now / he thinks / dragging his feet towards the

rickety-looking aircraft / folding his lanky frame into the little plane . . . / Aidy stops typing to pick up & re-pin a Polaroid that has fallen down / it's a snap of him & his three kids / Leo / Osh / & Eimear / taken in the garden last summer using Osh's fancy camera / tacks it back to the centre of his pin board / studies it for a second & smiles / despite the lingering sting of his right fist / Aidy pounds the keys of his laptop furiously / punches in plosive-heavy vocabulary / compound adjectives & dynamic verbs / powerful-sounding words / feels like a boxer swinging for his opponent / & landing the big ones / word count going up & up / after a sweaty first couple of rounds finding his range / jabbing at the keys / navigating the mind games / he gets to the end of another paragraph / exhales / deeply / a breath he didn't even know he was holding in & has another sip of his drink / searches for aeroplane cabin white noise on Spotify / as a United fan / knows about the Busby Babes / has watched plane crashes on YouTube for weeks / subscribed to FlightChannel / watched the animated reconstructions of Chapecoense / Germanwings / Vichai Srivaddhanaprabha in that helicopter in Leicester / difficult watches / death after death / things going wrong / dreaded tension / the inevitability of impact / of death / of bodies / anxiety-inducing tragedies / avoidable / usually / the result of human error / or overconfidence / incompetence or naivety / or some kamikaze mission / he finds the video he needs / one he has watched many times before / about the footballer / a version of his main character / watches / pauses / writes a few lines / resumes / repeats / fleshes out hints of his backstory / a seemingly ordinary Argentinian upbringing / made steady progress as a schoolboy before being spotted by a scout / by twenty he had made it to Europe plying his trade in France / not really fitting in to begin / hardly excelling / a gangly centre-forward / a route-one target man / far from prolific in front of goal in those early years / but certainly a hard worker / a loyal teammate / a selfless asset / & as the little plane prepares for take-off he's nervous / still a bit

unsure about this sudden uprooting / signing for a
team he doesn't really know / he'd never even heard
of a few weeks ago / deep down / in his heart of
hearts / he's still not sure if he wants to go / is quite
happy where he is / doing well in France now / has
settled / found his feet / joint top goalscorer this
season / but after weeks of talks / he's been drawn
away / persuaded to play in the Premier League /
has had his arm twisted by his agent / & his agent's
contacts / friends of friends / has boarded this
ramshackle plane / flown by this British pilot for
this trip across the Channel / he writes lines about
all this / Aidy does / being fast & loose with the
truth / using fact to flesh out the fiction / tries to
'show' / not 'tell' / still doesn't confidently know
what that means but hopes it involves keeping his
sentences short / tries to maintain the pace / but
still have deep moments in there too / moments
that will really resonate / add emotion / that says
something deep about the world / fear / grief / love
/ family / then suddenly / as sudden as a sneeze /
Aidy starts / as he so often does these days / to

think about his own family / his birth mother in particular / & the events from back in 1956 / the year of his birth / that led him here / to this moment sitting at his dining table in this house he lives in alone trying to write about tragedy / trying to piece bits together of the mystery / straining to see / peeking through lace-curtained Irish history / he remembers / how could he ever forget? / being young & never feeling worthy / wanted / called all sorts at the school gates / by other children in the playground / teachers in the classroom / words he didn't always understand / remembers being beaten blacker & blue by firm-fisted bullies / older children offended by the colour of his skin / his off-white blackish blemish / the kink of his afro / & despite their taunts / & threats of violence / no-one doing anything about it / doing anything to help / & having no birth mum to run to / for years he kept it in / bottled it up / a family did eventually have him / swoop in / & they were lovely / the best foster family he could have asked for in the circumstances / but as the years went by he realised / despite their

love / he still had to look after number one / &
that's when he started doing what he could to just
survive / learned to fight / had to / & in doing so /
despite his best intentions / unintentionally started
conforming to a level of violence expected of him in
the name of self-defence / took up boxing the
summer before starting high school / doing what he
needed to do to stay alive long enough to see *her*
again one day / his birth mother / he has tried /
spent many nights searching deep within himself to
remember something / anything at all of her to
help him with his search / but it's hard / memory
splintered-glass fragile / he often beats himself up /
curses his lack of recall / even though he knows he
was just eleven months / still just a baby / thinks of
her always / the woman who brought him into this
world / what she would have gone through at the
time / he grew old enough quickly enough to hear
the rumours / cryptic half-truths about how he
ended up where he did / when he did / the lofty
family reputation she had to protect / the times at
the time / meaning / in the circumstances / she had

no choice really / no chance of keeping him / even if
she wanted to / having got pregnant while
unmarried / & of all things / to a black man / but he
doesn't know exactly what parts / if any / are true /
his life a collage of unsourced stories / broken bits
& pieces / fragmented scraps / that's all he has to
cling on to / he spends his days now just looking for
those missing pieces / the history of his backstory /
he knows there are many others like him who never
find the truth / their long-lost mothers / histories
burden-bearers / often / out in town / in Erneside /
at a wedding / or yet another funeral of an old
friend / a distant cousin or someone might hint at
knowing something / & even now / Aidy can't help
but get his hopes up a little bit

/ / /

he often wonders what she might be doing / is she a
good cook? / does she have a sweet tooth? / does she
watch *EastEnders*? / does she have other children?
/ did she ever find love? / the things that shape a

19

person / he wrote her a letter / finally got a lucky break you could say / after years of trying / decades of digging / hoping & praying / he got an address / & after the most agonising of waits / it felt like he was finally getting somewhere / gratefully received from an unexpected source / breathless snippets from his uncle / practically on his deathbed / seems he was sworn to secrecy / by who Aidy doesn't know / took what he knew to his grave / literally / & in his condition / those final moments before the lights went out / didn't seem entirely confident / Aidy's dying uncle / as he gingerly scrawled a few lines / & a postcode / barely legible / but at least it was something / he had an address / of sorts / that night / back at home in Belleek / Aidy was brave enough to put pen to paper more or less straight away / sat solemn at the kitchen table / words straight from the heart jotted down in bold black biro / & once he started / the words came gushing out / poured onto the page like tears

Dear mother,

I have no doubt you will be surprised or may be
upset to receive this letter. I hope you will be happy.
I am not sure? I have received little and conflicting
information over the last 40 years or so. I will not
go into too much detail in case you do not wish to
contact me, I did provide your brother, my uncle, a lot
of information. Sadly he died earlier this afternoon.

I have since met my father in Grenada and I have
come to realise that life is too short and we are not
getting any younger and we will have regrets that we
never met should anything happen to either of us.
I have left things for so long hoping that you may
change your mind about meeting me.

Should you wish to contact me I have left my home
address, email (all lower case) and mobile number.

Your son, Aidy . . .

p.s. I do not blame you for the situation that you
found yourself back in the fifties, the world and
attitudes have changed since then . . . I hope

despite that thrilling initial rush / Aidy agonised
about whether to actually send it for weeks / months
/ what felt like years / but he finally built up the
courage last November / special delivery / but even
to this day . . . nothing / not even a hint of a reply /
Aidy knows that with all the endless postal strikes
/ cyber-security glitches / post-Brexit international
postage issues / catfishing & phishing scams / & all
that sort of thing / there's no guarantee that she
actually received it / there's a chance that maybe it's
still en route / in a sorting office somewhere still
being . . . sorted / still being put in the right bag
to be put into the right van to be posted through
the right door / or it might have been lost / fallen
down some crack / some cobwebbed crevice / to be
discovered in a decade or two by some overworked
underpaid cleaner / or maybe she's randomly
relocated / moved since his uncle's / her brother's
/ passing / sought pastures new out of the city
completely / or left England altogether / he's
thought / many times / about flying over / going
to the address he was given / nearly went the next

day / but stopped himself / hasn't yet built up the
courage / doesn't quite have it in him / as much as
he's desperate to meet her . . . deep inside there's
something holding him back / a deep-rooted fear
forcefully preventing him / terrified she'll reject him

/ / /

focus Aidy / fucking focus! / this is not the time
for self-pitying sentimental snowflake bullshit /
he thinks to himself / channel that soppy gushing
emotional stuff into this / right here / right now / at
this dining room table / on this laptop / this *is what
matters* / he says / smacking his forehand with the
edge of his palm / focus Aidy! / he writes another
line / a simple sentence to build momentum / opens
a new tab / Google / again / looks up a Nantes shirt
with the number nine on the back / keen to take
this research seriously / give this project the level
of dedication it deserves / it wouldn't arrive for
another few weeks it seems / long after the deadline
/ but this project here / he thinks / this could be

23

more than just a short story for this competition
/ this has bigger potential / a novella / a novel /
film rights? / words taking on a new lease of life
off the back of the ending of someone else's / but
the shirt is too expensive / he decides / & closes the
tab / then / as so often happens / he thinks of *her*
again / his birth mother / he never doesn't really /
Googles 'Greenford' / where he was told she lives
/ or at least lived / the images make it look leafy
/ not the London he imagined / he plops the little
orange street-view man on the Broadway / imagines
his old girl trundling along with her shopping
trolley / bartering with the butchers / bantering
with the bank managers / buying ciggies from the
newsagent's / trundling onto one of the buses / the
E6 or the 105 / clutching a little coin purse & keeps
her bus pass somewhere secret / somewhere safe /
he wonders if she thinks about him as often as he
does her / then thankfully / before it starts to hurt
too much / his thoughts return to here / to now / to
Belleek / to sitting at the dining room table in front
of his laptop with lines to write / a story to confront

/ head on / he did all the work to this place himself
/ knocked down walls / laid the flooring / has been
working on the garden too / it's all finally starting
to come together / starting to look the part / be a
home to be proud of / smacks his head again / with
his good hand / suddenly annoyed with himself
for getting distracted / derailed / again / clicks back
onto the Word doc / his untitled project-in-progress
/ reads back his last line / it's fine / enough to keep
him going / so he writes the next / then one more
/ every little helping / his main character / not
particularly well-known / yet / but is now on his
way from France to the UK / meetings & paperwork
/ contract & clauses / the deal has been done & the
character's fate has been sealed / soon he will be
lining up against Manchester United / Manchester
City / Chelsea / Liverpool / Arsenal / in the biggest
league in the world / Aidy pauses / stretches / braces
himself / there's a big scene coming up / knows how
deep he will have to go to get this right / the locked
black screen of his iPhone a shadowy unlit mirror /
catches a glimpse of himself at an unflattering angle

/ feels old / frumpy / ugly / sees deep cavernous
wrinkles like old wounds / battle scars / he pinches
at his cheeks / prods his protruding chin / breathes
right in / come on Aidy / time to crack on / but
before he restarts he opens a tab / looks up flights
to Argentina / closes it shortly after / *This is useless*
/ he says to himself / aloud / you'll never get this
published / he thinks to himself / don't be stupid / if
you're lucky / he thinks / by some miracle maybe /
some slither of a slim chance / if you're lucky / the
best you can expect is some start-up independent
press / he says to himself / a proper dodgy one /
don't expect any money up front / his thoughts
continue / more likely to be someone just saying
*yeah, go on then* as a joke / someone pressing print
for a laugh / it won't sell / it will sit unread on
bookshelves / gathering dust just like his poetry
pamphlets / picked up promisingly by a possible
punter / blurb skimmed / eyebrows raised / but
then it'll be put back / Tadgh from A Novel Idea in
Ballyshannon will update him every time he pops
in / report that still none have been sold since he

last asked last week / eventually unflogged copies
are returned / it will sit dusty in pongy libraries
/ no-one will come to his book-signing slot / he
imagines an old lady waddling over / purely out
of pity really / ask *What's it about?* / & then say
*Well good luck with it, dear* / & waddle off again
/ you won't be invited to the big book festivals /
you won't sit on panels with esteemed guests / no
chance / getting more irate Aidy writes another
line as the little plane from his story begins to
struggle / describes clouds at night / wants to say it
looks like floating candy floss / knows that sounds
too twee / describes them instead as translucent &
troublesome / describes the worsening weather /
the up & down / twists & turns / the storm-tossed
plane starting to wrestle & writhe against the
elements / stuttering through night-darkened skies
/ bumbling along / tripping & tumbling / slipping
& stumbling / rolling with the rough & tumble /
the fizz & bang / everything feeling much too tight
/ as the little aircraft lumbers on all lopsided / the
up / the up / the up / the down / down / down / the

hazy horizon / ink-splat sky / little plane a target
in a game of dodgeball staggering through a coffee-
black tunnel of darkness / it's blackout-blind dark /
slate-grey sky turning abysmally black / the only
light the footballer sees is the odd ship from the
Channel below / the pilot whose language Aidy's
main character doesn't really understand muttering
something concerning / unnerving / the low wing
wobbling in the wind / trudging through the thick
fog of cloud / wading in it / jaws clenched / toes tense
/ neck sore / shoulders heavy / should flying a plane
look *this* hard? / he wonders / Aidy's main character
/ staring at the man at the controls / hoping he's got
this under control / but not looking entirely at ease
/ not at all really / once you've done all the training
/ sat the exams / clocked the hours / is it still hard? /
day to day? / to Aidy's backseat passenger it looks it
/ immensely so / Aidy ponders all this as he writes /
line after line / ending one page & starting at the top
of a new one / on a bit of a roll now

/ / /

Aidy thinks of flights he's taken down the years
/ both good & bad trips / all those sharp angles &
tight turns / the spotting of swimming pools &
tennis courts coming in to land / then returns to
his story / the little plane with the footballer at the
back performing stomach-lurching manoeuvres
through canopies of clouds / lawnmower loud /
Aidy's main character / valued at fifteen million
pounds apparently / now just a sitting duck in a
smoke-clogged plane / hiccupping into the dark
via the backstreets of the unknown / Aidy cracks
his fingers / slurps his Guinness / downs the last
crumbs of his second packet of crisps / it's just gone
seven & he's nearly reached a thousand words /
feels proud / does a little celebratory jig in his seat
/ a little bum-shaking wiggle / is just about to get
himself another bag of crisps when he suddenly
hears the closeness of a car which startles him / a
low hum followed by the familiar crunch of tyres
on gravel / with a quick glance at the CCTV screen
behind him / he sees there's someone pulling into
his drive / a flash-looking thing / & it dawns on him

who it is & why they're here / how could he get
it wrong? / how could he forget? / his designated
weekend with his daughter / his youngest child of
the three / Eimear / & as she & her mum get out
/ he hastily shuts his laptop / then opens it again
to make sure he has saved the newest version of
his story / just in case / then rushes to the door to
greet them / swinging it open just before they're
about to knock / *Hey!* / he says / a little flustered /
suddenly a little self-conscious of the Tayto-y tang
of his cheese & onion breath / as he goes in for a
kiss / then a hug / both of which are awkwardly
dodged by the woman in her early fifties at Aidy's
door / her hair that was clearly once red / now
more straw-coloured & greying / gracefully / she
is wearing a face full of make-up / looks glamorous
/ looks beautiful / still / *Hey, you!* / Aidy says /
addressing the tall teenage girl at the older woman's
side / curly brown hair / colour in her cheeks /
Eimear / the Guinness is already going to his head
& he has to stop himself ruffling the top of her scalp
like she's a Labrador / she's sixteen in a few weeks

/ *Hey, Dad* / she says / shy / unsure / eyes to the
ground / as she toes her once-white Air Forces that
she begged Aidy for less than six months ago / he
couldn't see the appeal personally / even though he
had seen literally every teenager in town wearing
them / the soles were far too thick / & why they
didn't make the actual tick itself stand out more /
make it a different colour at least / he doesn't know
/ surely it would make more sense / given the price
/ to make the brand bolder than it was / he didn't
say anything of course as he parted with his cash
at the till / he is more than aware that the age gap
between them is unusually big / especially compared
to some of her school friends / he can't deny it /
Eimear's hesitancy at the doorstep saddens him /
this is not how he imagined / or hoped / fatherhood
to be / seeing her for just a couple of days every few
weeks / & her still seeming a little unsure around
him all these years after the divorce / he makes
an effort to attend school plays & hockey games /
parents' evening & birthdays / but it's not always
been easy to get the time off work / in the past /

or when he has / it's still so awkward between him
& Siobhan the whole vibe's off / making it hard to
shake the feeling he isn't really wanted there / Aidy
wishes it was different / *Come in, come in . . . I'll
put the kettle on* / gesturing the both of them inside
as he slyly turns up the dial on the thermostat /
*No, no . . . I can't stay, Darragh is taking me for
dinner tonight* / Aidy eyes wide-open sting / saliva
too clumpy-thick to swallow as he hears the click of
the boiler rumbling on behind him / stirring into
action / he knew of course she wouldn't come in /
she never does / never accepts an offer of a coffee
/ cup of tea / glass of wine / *Oh, I see, anywhere
nice?* / over Siobhan's shoulder Aidy spots the spiky
brown dot of a hedgehog / an odd time to be out
/ *Just somewhere in Bundoran like, it's our one-
year anniversary* / she says decisively / something
inside him pin-prick pinches / first on the surface
then somewhere much deeper / what could have
been, eh? / Aidy thinks / Siobhan made motherhood
look easy / took to it the first time better than Aidy
the third / had no problems setting boundaries /

routines / ruthless in actually enforcing them /
no dummy / limits on screen time / a keen eye on
sugar & salt intake / that sort of thing / Eimear
is the product of Siobhan's meticulous systems /
diligent / vigilant / mild-mannered & bookish /
smashing it at school / captain of the hockey team /
wants to be a scientist or an Olympian or both she
says / however frosty their relationship at times /
Eimear will always be the beautiful by-product of
a sometimes tricky relationship / Aidy didn't find
marriage easy / the first or third time / didn't expect
to experience the emotional extremes as intensely
as he did / that initial blissful high / the really low
lows / the constant pressure to perform allowing
dark thoughts to creep in / causing self-diagnosed
depression / the weight of the role too much to take
at times / felt it almost daily / a load that got heavier
/ a constant court-martialled guilt of not being a
good life partner / the mis-management of money /
less & less intimacy / feeling like he always needed
to perform on the increasingly seldom occasions
they were intoxicated enough to touch each other

/ he didn't expect to hate this apparent need to
provide all the time / physically / financially / but
emotionally too / sometimes he just wanted to lock
himself away / the garage / the 'man shed' down
the road / pub on the outskirts of town / take the
longer route home / just to feel like himself again
for an hour or so / be himself again for a little while
/ nursing a flat pint in the corner / reading the paper
in the car / he knows he wasn't always there at
dinner / or around to put them to bed & read them
a story / deliberately so / regrets it all now / knows
he could have done better / tried harder / he doesn't
want to make excuses / it wasn't good enough / *he*
wasn't good enough / but a part of him thinks not
having his birth mum or dad around made it harder
to believe in the idea of family / in the functional
sense at least / he hadn't seen how it should be done
/ how to make it work even when things got tough
/ *OK love, be good, see you on Sunday* / Siobhan
says / as she gives her only daughter a little peck on
her cheek before pacing it back to her shiny black
Audi / so swanky it makes Aidy's relatively new

Qashqai look shit / *Have a lovely dinner! I'll drop her off sometime in the afternoon* / Aidy shouts / desperately keen to seem pleased for her as she hops in / not saying anything / reversing out of the drive / his drive / with a little more effort than should be needed because of Aidy's bad parking from earlier / he sees her raise a firm hand / a rough-edged goodbye / not quite a wave / more of a salute / as she pulls out of the driveway

/ / /

throughout the years / largely because of the age gap between them / their relationship was the talk of the town / gossip-mongering locals poking their noses in / then when it came to an end / ran its course / they were the first to blame him for the failure of the marriage / accusing him of failing Eimear & the rest of his children / thankfully for Aidy / of late at least / the community interest in his love life is dwindling / their prying quietening / it's not like he didn't try with Siobhan / he thinks he did / but just felt this constant pressure to make the marriage work / especially after two failed attempts previously / expectation weighed too heavy / felt it every hour of every day / so desperate to make it all right / he got it all wrong / despite his best efforts to do all he could to be a good husband / especially as a man of colour / he was far from comfortable with what people expected of him / of the marriage / he was a Black man / of course he was bound to run away as soon as things got hard / of course he couldn't keep it in his trousers / of course he was a fork-tongued cheat / would shag anything in a skirt / when in all truth / it wasn't like that at all / as Aidy steps inside it already feels like the heating's kicking in / Eimear stands awkwardly in the middle of the sitting room / as if waiting for instruction / as if she's never set foot here before / she looks over her left shoulder / then looks over her right / thinks about sitting down but needs prompting / *Give us your coat, Eimear, love* / he didn't take the news he was going to be a father for the third time very well / barely coped the first two times / terrified by the prospect of even less sleep than he was struggling to achieve already / the middle-of-the-night bottle feed / the vomming / the weaning / the teething / the never-ending lesson-learning / cupboards crammed with Calpol / unidentifiable slop plopped on his white sock / it felt like starting again / & the first two attempts weren't that much of a success / *You must be hungry?* / Aidy says / suddenly worrying there's nothing in / but to his relief / from the back of the freezer / behind half a bag of peas / he digs out a three-cheese Chicago Town pizza / not something Aidy would have bought for himself / probably something Osh got / but he's glad to find something other than the Bombay Bad Boy Pot Noodle he had planned for himself this evening / Aidy preheats the oven / scrapes ice clumps off the back of the box to read the cooking instructions / *So, how was school today, love?* / he winces inside / instantly regrets not coming up with a better way to untangle the tension / this strained strangeness that lingers in the gap between Aidy in the kitchen & Eimear in the living room sitting at the edge of

the settee untying her shoelaces / *Fine* / she replies
/ Aidy knows she's doing well / a student all the
teachers adore / has witnessed first-hand all the
praise heaped on her at parents' evening / read the
reports / polite / well-behaved / homework always
done on time / to the highest standard / a future
hockey star / has sat in the stands when he could
get the time off / knows she has that fire in her
belly when on the field / barking out instructions /
cajoling underperforming teammates / bamboozling
opponents with quick feet / dizzying defenders
with all the skill & speed needed to get into match-
winning positions / but this same fire she shows
mid-match is not present at all right now as she
silently unzips her rucksack / takes out a well-
thumbed book that Aidy can't quite see & begins
to read / *Any matches coming up?* / he asks as he
pops the pizza in the oven / she's tall for her age /
shoots up well above all the others in her class / as
she swivels in her seat a little to answer him / he can
see it's a book by Sally Rooney / he's not much of
a reader of modern stuff / dabbles more with non-

fiction really / history books & that / bit of poetry of course too / but Eimear looks about halfway through / & the pages are being turned quickly / *What do you want to do this evening, love? We've still got that* Line of Duty *finale to watch . . .* / she doesn't look up at this suggestion / not in a rude way / Aidy hopes at least / just completely absorbed by her book / *. . . or we could play that guessing game, with the little cards we played with your brothers last Christmas, what's it called again? Codenames? Bought the two-player version in town the other day . . .* / she doesn't look up from her book / Aidy isn't sure whether she's just thinking about what to reply or whether she just doesn't care / couldn't actually think of something worse than playing silly board games with her father on a Friday / or both / he perseveres / *Tomorrow, I'm thinking we go for a walk around Castle Caldwell, I've not been for ages, what d'ya think?* / surprisingly this suggestion appears to go down better than the idea of playing Codenames / at least he gets a little nod in reply this time / Aidy isn't sure why / wouldn't call it a

resounding *yes* but certainly not a *no* either / &
Aidy is buoyed by her indifference / progress

/ / /

he's had enough of just having himself for company
most days / Osh comes / dumps more of his stuff
& goes / & don't get him started on Leo / there's
no-one really here for him / he feels so lonely of
late he's sought comfort online / *Hurry! Aidy ♥*
*Ukrainian girls are looking for true love ♥* / the first
email said / a panicked Aidy thought his increased
porn-watching in recent weeks was to blame for this
message sneaking into his main inbox / by simply
receiving it he was sure that someone somewhere
was somehow watching him even though he had
turned off all his cookies / whatever that meant /
& put a sticker over his camera / he panicked / &
deleted the message straight away / emphatically
slammed his laptop shut & vowed to not go on
anymore dodgy sites again / old DVDs would
have to do for when he got desperate / but as the

weeks went by more emails followed / he clicked
on it accidentally / he told himself initially / then
deliberately the second & third times & within just a
few hours of scrolling / then inputting some details
/ had started speaking to a girl from Kiev / said
her name was Kateryna / twenty-seven / swapped
WhatsApps / & deep down inside he knows he's
being swindled / conned / emotionally manipulated
/ but the steady stream of private messages from a
busty blonde twenty-something declaring her love
for him / however untrue / does something to stop
some of the sadness that gets harder & harder to
handle / he has given up hope of finding real love
again / he's had his shot / three times & more

/ / /

Aidy plates up & starts to set up *Line of Duty* on
the TV in the living room / Eimear folds over the
corner of her page & starts poking her pinky at the
undercooked crust of her overdone pizza / after a
few little bites she puts her plate down on the coffee

table / *Dad, I'm tired, can I just go to bed?* / a big
blow / it's only seven thirty & he had been looking
forward to watching the finale with his daughter
for weeks / dodging all the spoilers at work / & on
Facebook / *Of course, sweetheart, you have my
bed* / he says wishing he tidied up the spare room
a bit after Osh / *Have you got your pyjamas?* / a
question which seems to mildly irritate her / she
hitches her rucksack over a single shoulder / the
weight heavy for just a weekend / bulky with the
weight of more books perhaps / Aidy wonders
whether to go in for a kiss as she shuffles closer to
say *Goodnight* / holds back / holds off / waits for
her to give him something / a flicker / an inch / gets
a little hug instead / distanced / *Love you* / he says
/ either Eimear doesn't hear or chooses not to as she
silently scurries upstairs / pacing up the steps two at
a time / from below Aidy hears her skittering about
/ & then after a few moments / settling into bed /
his bed / & he basks in the creak of movement above
him / the reassurance of having her here / in his
home / if only for the weekend / he switches off the

TV / will save *Line of Duty* for another day / pours
himself his third Guinness of the evening / sidles
towards the dining table / opens his laptop / clicks
his fingers / finds his place again & begins to type


/ / /


he reacquaints himself with the voice of his main
character / relearns the language of the frightened
footballer / who himself / in time / hopes to learn
the language of the pilot who's muttering something
unsettling / there's something definitely wrong /
journey not going how it should be / the smoke-
belching plane wobbling increasingly unsteady /
shaking erratically in the stormy purgatory above
the Channel / like a footy fan on an away day who's
had too much to drink / anxiety-fuelling flashing
red light from one of the wings / flash / flash / flash
/ he feels bone-deep tired / inexplicably exhausted
/ drained / breathless / watery weak / it's been an
energy-sapping sleep-depriving last few days packing
& preparing but now he feels like he's properly

struggling / airways tightening / like hands around
his neck / throttling him / gripping tighter & tighter
/ he glances out from the black of the sky then down
into the black of the sea / the invisibility of the
unknown / nothing but the unseen underneath as
they judder through January skies / not soaring /
not flying as high as they should be in an old tatty-
looking plane that has clocked up too many miles /
a clapped-out 'cuckoo' / a dodgy fucking rust-bucket
/ an unworthy / unairworthy dinger / a decrepit
piece of shit no longer fit for purpose / whining
wild / an angle-grinding drone / then a deafening
whistling / deathly quiet / then suddenly / deathly
LOUD / this little plane is doing its best to dodge
the clouds / ducking & diving / bopping & weaving
/ the frightened footballer knows it's not looking
good / can see it / can smell it / can feel it / he opens
WhatsApp & records a voice message:

Hey brothers . . . how's everything going? Brother,
I'm dead. I was in Nantes doing stuff, stuff, stuff and
stuff. Never-ending, never-ending, never-ending,

never-ending. So anyway, boys . . . I'm now on a
plane which seems . . . *about to fall apart* and now
I'm leaving for Cardiff. Crazy that tomorrow I'll be
training in the afternoon with my new teammates . . .
We'll see what happens. So how are things with you,
brothers? All well? In an hour and a half if you haven't
had news of me . . . I don't know if they'll send
someone to look for me, because they're not going to
find me . . . but . . . you know . . . I'm so scared . . .

Aidy is moved by it all / the fear in his voice / the
pure desperation / but four words strike him / hard
/ right in his heart / right where it hurts / . . . about
to fall apart . . . / he scrolls up to the first page of
his Word document / drops the cursor before his
first word & writes **ABOUT TO FALL APART**
in big bold block capitals / he has a title / he has
*his* title / he feels joyful & petrified / this project
is actually coming to life / feels real now / line by
line / with every passing minute / he plays music
to celebrate / Einaudi / & as 'Luminous' starts his
fingers frantically type / it's getting intense in the

45

cockpit / the plane is proper struggling / wiggling
& wobbling in the night sky / twisting & turning
/ the rain pelting down / lightning flashing strobe-
light bright / thunder rumbling headphone-loud /
little plane zigzagging around cloud in its attempts
to get away / break free / get to Blighty in one piece
/ performing stomach-churning lurches every other
second as it veers further & further off course / as it
begins to make an unscheduled toe-curling descent /
trying to outmanoeuvre the clouds / weaving right
/ weaving left / meandering miles away from the
nearest runway / miles away from the safety of the
British south coast / all sounds & senses intensified /
ear-splittingly loud / a drug-heavy rave in someone's
fourth-floor flat he doesn't want to be at / bleeping
& flashing / bleeping & flashing / piercing much
too sharp / & pilot muttering things he does not
understand / clearly panicked / manically pressing
buttons / tugging at levers frantically / the engine is
rattling rusty / a broken chainsaw set to the wrong
speed / the noise hurting / throbbing / drilling into
his brain / eyes dropping / beginning to close / not

46

seeing is not believing / temporarily not being / a
fleeting much-needed respite / his head tight & taut
as the plane turns & turns / trying to outfly Mother
Nature & failing / falling / dipping lower & lower
/ this was not how it was meant to be / to end? /
from sun-drenched Argentina / to Brittany / to right
here / a living nightmare / not flying as high as he
should be / pilot punching buttons / turning to his
main character / bracing him for the inevitable / in
words not understood / language a barrier / flailing
/ failing to control the plane / he's trying everything
he can . . . but it's too late / things look desperately
bad / events turning terribly sad / man down / down
/ Aidy needs to get all this down

down

down

down . . .

# SATURDAY

AS THE SUN STARTS TO RISE AIDY BOLTS UPRIGHT /
clothes drenched / soaked head to torso with sweat /
he wonders for a moment where he is / wonders how
he's found himself here / wonders why his whole
body aches & his head hurts / he looks around &
gradually finds his bearings again / it seems Aidy
didn't make it to bed last night / which would have
been the sofa anyway with Eimear upstairs / instead
/ he fell asleep right here at his desk / working on
his story till god knows what time / he frantically
prods at his phone screen / sees a flurry of messages
from Kateryna / ignores them for now / although
constantly worried about her given what's happening
over there / doesn't have the heart to play pretend
this morning / he will message back later / he
promises to himself / he yawns / he stretches / he
stands / he curses / he sits back down / he thought

about it / toyed with the idea for months / but
decided not to splash out building a separate study
/ a proper swanky little writing space / felt selfish
somehow / silly / & after doing all the work around
the house over the last few years / there isn't much
left to spare now anyway / so he writes here at the
dining table instead / in between the kitchen & the
living room / on the table stacked high with letters &
bills & random bits of ID / things that need sorting
out sorted into different piles / for ease / no space to
eat really / but he has shuffled things around a bit /
just enough / to make room for his laptop / not ideal
but it will have to do / no time to make excuses / he
has all he needs to get this done / an idea / a laptop
/ & as soon as the kettle is boiled . . . a much-needed
coffee to wake himself up / he closes his Hotmail /
retrieves a lens wipe from his stash / wipes down
the keys / fingers the gunky crevices / it's just after
seven / the main road through Belleek library-quiet
/ & despite falling asleep on the job last night /
Aidy has woken up feeling surprisingly lighter /
sufficiently refreshed at least to crack on / ready to

flesh out more of the distressed mother / desperate
to find her footballer son / it's been two days since
his main character went missing / vanished into mid-
air mid-flight / spluttering through the night sky
from Nantes to Cardiff / despite months of research
/ Aidy doesn't know very much about *her* story / in
real life / so imagines her ordeal / the all-consuming
pain / he gets up & goes for a piss / brushes his
teeth / makes his hot drink / returns to his desk
/ interlocks his fingers / clicks them awake & sets
out to work / a couple of days have passed since the
plane disappeared / vanished / but to her what she's
heard simply isn't true / it's fake news / reports of
the little plane careering into the English Channel /
made up / a fabricated fairytale / her son *is* still alive
/ somewhere / clinging desperately on to a craggy
rock in the cold sea / or clutching on to a floating
bit of debris / just waiting for someone to help / it's
just a case of tracking him down using all the latest
technology / plucking him up like one of those claws
at an arcade / or a digger from a building site / dust
him down / clean him off / & bring him home /

back into her arms / she is not prepared to entertain
the ever-growing concern that he has gone for
good / accept that she might not ever see her baby
boy again / Aidy writes this all down / writes till it
gradually starts to feel less awful / less clunky / till
the lines feel more natural in a voice that feels more
assured / thinking again about all the plane journeys
he's taken / the sensations of take-off / flying /
landing / using memory to flesh out sensory details
/ he usually finds flying a faff but he's gone on a fair
few flights down the years / he's been to Australia
many times / even lived there for a while / has more
air miles than many / was over there recently in fact
/ a family wedding a few months ago / a relative of
his foster family / he remembers a young girl sitting
in front of him losing an AirPod / how lucky! / some
people have lost their son / & their mums / as the
plane prepared for landing someone else fainted /
laid flat out on the aisle of the plane / sugar levels
low / he overheard someone say / Aidy pitter-patter
types to try & convey that fearsome thrill of flying
/ as well-travelled as he is / despite all those flights

taken down the years / despite where he works now
& has worked before / take-off still makes his toes
curl / catapulting into the air all askew somehow still
feels unnatural / & the thump of the wheels hitting
the tarmac still makes his heart leap / he gets it all
down / watches the number at the bottom left corner
go up & up & up & smiles / the words gushing
out of him / he's had this idea for months / & it's
showing / he remembers hearing the original story
on the radio / remembers how it stopped him in his
tracks / remembers feeling moved / frozen still / a
tragic tale of two men losing their lives completely
unnecessarily / plane crashes happen all the time /
Aidy knows that more than most / but something
struck him cold about this particular tragedy / so he
writes & writes / does everything he can to bring
the story to life / hasn't yet worked out the ending
/ not fully / he'll get there when he gets there / he
thinks / reassuring himself / has a rough idea at the
back of mind somewhere maybe / on his way to &
from work he's been listening to the podcasts about
the crash / & then the investigation / read the odd

article about what happened / flicked through a few
books / feels like a detective some days / piecing it
all together / & now it's just a case of getting it down
/ adding more & more words / despite how cringe
they seem / he knows he can't edit words that aren't
there to begin with / he's trying to stay positive /
feels right in the thick of it now / & he's determined
to make this work / the mother / who remains
nameless / wanders around her house in northern
Argentina aimlessly / in the kitchen / then the living
room / out into the garden & then back in again /
touching every surface her son once did / gripping
bannisters & table edges for support / there to break
her sudden fall if needed to / everything reminds
her of him / thinking about meals she would cook
/ & although her family rarely leave her side / she
still feels autumn-leaf brittle / unsteady & unable
to hold it together / always *about to fall apart* / her
ex-husband / her son's dad / is trying his best / but
the limbo of the unknown is taking its toll on him
too / worse probably / & when he goes to hug her
/ console her / in the huddle of their embrace / a

coming together weighty with their shared history
/ unsteadied by the uncertainty of the future / two
people not as close as they once were / now closer
than ever / they strain / they shake / they shatter /
the trembling makes them tumble / the dad falling
to the floor in a heap / he writes it all down / Aidy
does / determined to actually finish a project for once
/ even booked a flying lesson at St Angelo the other
week / all part of the research to add authenticity
/ even with 'mate's rates' still cost quite a bit for
an hour in the sky / but after a couple of drinks in
Enniskillen one evening it felt worth it / he thought
/ for the sake of the project / & he was nervous
before take-off / shit scared in fact as he clambered
into the little four-seat Cessna / but you know what
/ he actually felt alright once up there / took the
controls for a bit too / only for a couple of minutes
or so / but it was enough

/ / /

in Aidy's story / the second part of three follows

the footballer's mum in the weeks after losing
her son / the now confirmed tragedy of his death
felt raw / the heart-heavy aftermath still scalpel-
sharp / the however many stages of grief all felt at
once / he's aiming for two thousand words for this
part / two thousand words to depict the mother's
incomprehension of what's happened / the outrage
/ the hope it's all some kind of dream / the gut-
wrenching grief / life has just gone on since the
death of her son & now there is new news that has
taken its place / matches played without him / shops
opening for business / babies being born / life just
going on / tentative talks of inquests / judicial jargon
she doesn't understand / to them nothing's changed
/ to her / her world has ended / he gets it all down
/ Aidy has been told before that sensory language
is key / that he does understand / not just what can
be seen but what can be heard too / trying to make
his scenes feel real / vivid & claustrophobic / capture
the smell of grief / how it reeks / stinks / lingers for
days & weeks / the stench of loss seeping into her
skin / soaking into her bones / he's keen to capture

how bereft it makes you feel / organless / empty /
barely living / but just about breathing / Aidy has
lost people before / countless friends & family /
but the grief that hurts the most to him / is the one
of his mother not wanting to find him / reunite /
his grief isn't linear / it's ongoing / undulating &
turbulent / hits hard like a brick to the brain / with
the pain travelling down & around the body so
much he doesn't want to leave his bed / or wake up
some mornings / doesn't see the point / his grief is
felt privately / mostly / but hers / the footballer's
mother / has gone viral / she's angry / furious / is
demanding justice / shouts for it / the world has
not stopped & taken stock of what has happened /
people board the bus / go to work / read the paper /
the football season continues / the minute's silence
well & truly over / black armbands yanked off &
flung away / she is sonless & nobody seems to care
/ the grief cuts her so deep she feels bludgeoned
by it / bleeding to death daily / over & over again
/ every time she wakes up / she feels deader than
the day before / images of her son's body have been

circulated / been made public / but not enough is
being done to bring him home / she thinks

/ / /

Aidy picks at the scab on his right hand / bits start to
flake free / he returns to his laptop / gets down more
lines / tries not to overthink / tries not to feel stupid
/ selfish / self-indulgent / as Aidy drags the cursor
up / he hears a car in his drive / he notices the time
/ shit he thinks / *Shit!* / he says / Aidy stands up /
brushes himself down & chucks in some gum found
buried in one of his pockets before rushing to the
door to let his younger son in / *Dad* / Osh says flatly
giving a little nod / straight-faced / it still stuns Aidy
to see his son standing so tall / flexing his bulging
biceps / much too tight muscle-fit t-shirt / voice
double-bass deep / facial hair filling out finally / acne
resolute / *Son!* / Aidy greets him too enthusiastically
/ as he goes in for a hug Osh keeps his arms down
by his side / *You got any food in? I'm starving* / Osh
asks / brushing past Aidy on a mission to fill his

belly / plonking his fancy leather washbag on the
counter / heading straight for the kitchen / before
Aidy has a chance to greet his sport-vest-wearing ex
Celeste . . . / she's already on the move / reversing
out of the drive / pulling out onto the main road &
speeding out of sight / not a hint of a glimpse back
/ if Aidy's relationship with Siobhan was messy /
his spell with Celeste bordered on toxic / *What's
the craic, lanky?* / Osh greets Eimear / who wobbles
in groggily having clearly just gotten up / & then
cracks the biggest smile Aidy has seen since she got
here last night as she runs to him / wraps her long
arms around her big brother / well . . . half-brother
/ *You're looking fit, son, been at the gym?* / Aidy
probes / poking him on the arm as Osh pulls the
fridge door open with wide eyes / eager hands / & a
rumbling tummy / Aidy has never really been Osh
levels of fitness-obsessed himself / not keen on doing
deadlifts / or Peloton-peddling along the west coast
/ taking selfies in Sondico sportswear bought from
Sports Direct / no chance / even less so now since
fucking his shoulder up after the crash the other

month / definitely needs surgery really / his body's
been through the wars really / did a bit of boxing
as a kid but injured his hand / had a promising
career too / could have gone pro / his sore fist now
is nothing compared to damage he's done in the past
/ *Not yet, maybe later . . . Parkrun in Enniskillen*
/ Osh replies / Aidy nods / *Oh yeah . . .* / even
though he doesn't have a clue what that is / *Ran with
Mum* / he adds / as he ruffles Eimear's hair to her
faux-annoyance / often Aidy wonders about how
different it could all be / if they were all one proper
family / something you see in the movies & on TV
/ children from the same mum / & yes / still having
to deal with the pressure of outgrown uniform /
after-school clubs / expensive enrichment trips /
university accommodation / graduation gowns / the
cost of living / energy bills & that / but at least being
all together / it all started to turn sour with Celeste
soon after the accident / the first one / up in the
air / while working on the rigs / not because of the
crash itself / but the messy aftermath / increasingly
heated conversations about compensation / will-

writing / shared savings accounts / it soon became
all that was discussed / an unsalvageable slippery
slope / a downwards spiral / arguments turned into
fights / not speaking to each other for days / weeks
/ kissless text messages / cold food in the microwave
/ or bunged in the oven / avoiding each other in the
kitchen / weighty talks / drunken fights / dreaded
amends / the inevitability of growing apart / love
still there / somewhere / but harder to find / at
least on her part anyway / regrets / regrets & an
empty fridge / there's not much in / mushrooms
shrivelling in plastic packaging / out-of-date bacon
discolouring / Osh yanks open the freezer & Aidy
hopes it's not for the pizza he & Eimear picked at
last night / but after a bit of digging / he finds some
bread that he starts to toast on a high heat instead /
*We could go to Castle Caldwell, have a walk round,*
*then grab some food afterwards?* / Aidy suggests /
unconfident / unsure / they both look at each other
/ Eimear & Osh / then after a brief pause / give a
little sheepish nod / a little indecisively / there are
better options / but this idea of being all together

somewhere *beautiful* has materialised in Aidy's mind
& settled there / they say *OK* / unconvincingly / but
it's enough to call it a green light / it's all systems
go as Osh butters his toast & takes a big bite / they
agree to get ready quickly & get going in twenty
minutes or so / in the bathroom that Aidy painted
& tiled himself / Osh's toothpaste-smeared washbag
perches at the edge of the sink & Aidy can't help
but take a peek / see the makings of the modern
man he's growing up to be / exfoliating face wash
& citrus-scented moisturiser & Brazilian Bum Bum
Cream & hair gel & charcoal teeth whitening &
aloe vera-scented dual-textured wet wipes / & more
stuff Aidy can't see / he zips it shut / he pisses / he
washes / sprays on some Old Spice / brushes his
teeth with his left hand / right still hurts / wiggles
on his trainers / locks the garage door / moments
later they clamber into the Qashqai / edge out onto
the main road / bellies rumbling like old pipes /
Osh is already connected to the car's Bluetooth /
already well-acquainted with how to get the music
playing / to Aidy's surprise his first choice is a pretty

catchy track / an Irish harp to start / a twinkly sound that lingers there in the background / it's still very young-sounding / pop-y with this kind of urban twist / a song that both Osh & Eimear seem to know / & like / judging by the light in their eyes / the subtle jutting of their jaw to the beat / he gives it a little while / enjoying the different textures of the song / including the young singer's vocals / before he asks / *Who's this, then?* / Aidy knows there's no way of asking about modern music without sounding like a dinosaur / as much as he tries to keep up / most songs these days blur into one / he tries to stay in the know / always got the radio on / blaring from his open garage for when he's pottering in the garden / or on the treadmill / or tinkering with this / that / or the other / but Aidy knows he's long in the tooth now / too old to keep up / *Gemma Dunleavy, 'Up De Flats'* / Osh replies / it's a good little song / it plays on repeat as they drive the fifteen minutes or so to Castle Caldwell / crossing the border / just / the bass of the beat filling the space

///

Aidy pulls into the near-empty car park / swings
into a spot & they all decamp at once / gearing
themselves up to walk the trail around the site
of the once stately home / Aidy knows the bare
bones of the castle's history / has read the signs
on previous visits / he's aware there's a connection
between its former owners & Belleek pottery / but
when here he likes to / as much as he possibly can
/ distance himself from its history / the sadness of
the story that has led to its state of disrepair / &
just appreciate the ruin for what it is now / fallen
apart but still / somehow / beautiful / as they begin
their undulating amble along the black trail / Aidy
forces a half-smile at the dogwalkers going the other
way as Eimear & Osh hurry ahead / guided by
the black arrows on the wooden signposts towards
Rossergole Point / this leisurely walk to them a
race / a challenge to the finish line / they tread the
gravel path / up the little inclines / down the slight
slopes / stones crunching underfoot / until what's

left of the actual castle gradually comes into view / Aidy has seen it before of course / many times / but is still taken aback by the sight of its current state / definitely seen better days / nothing more than a derelict shell now / damaged irreparably by decades of disrepair / the foliage has infiltrated the brick / every corner / infiltrating every crevice / nature taking hold / strangling the mortar into submission / fighting & winning / Aidy stands surveying the vastness of the ruins / the quiet of Lough Erne looming loud behind him / he stands / hands on hips / watching / imagining having the funds to restore this vast site to its former glory / showing love to something that for years has gone untouched / Channel 4 / Kevin McCloud / *Grand Designs* / rolled-up architect plans / rolled-up sleeves / roll-up ciggies & hard hats / articulated lorries squeezing down narrow country lanes / bullish Eastern European workforce / Aidy carries on along the path / his kids so far in front he can no longer see them / in the distance Aidy hears a dog / possibly the same one he walked past before

/ splashing about now somewhere causing ripples /
the water's heartbeat makes him think of his story
& the plane plunging into the water / & how / now /
the mum shuffles everywhere / lifelessly / unsteady
on her feet / standing-water deep / struggling to
move / struggling to breathe / she's sick / sore / &
tired / & doesn't know her next steps / what to do
next / as thoughts of the mum roll in & wash away
Aidy spots sprouting shamrock shining emerald
green sticking out of a rock / feels like he needs
all the luck he can get right now / then turns his
attention to the view / the only noise he hears now
is his stomach rumbling as he starts to trudge back
down along the path / suddenly feeling triggered by
the weight of memory / every now & then / down
the boozer or buying basics in Spar / someone will
mumble something / no louder than a whisper /
make some barbed-wire comment / will say he looks
a bit like Phil Lynott / or Paul McGrath / Aidy has
read McGrath's autobiography / read all about the
care homes / the borstals / the drinking / the dodgy
knees / a story that chimes with his own at times /

all of life's ups & down / the trauma & the tragedy
of being an Irish man of colour / but despite being of
a similar age / mixed-race / Irish mother / Black dad
/ McGrath's dad though / Aidy knows / is Nigerian
/ & now / only relatively recently mind you / knows
that his dad is in fact from the Caribbean

/ / /

Aidy booked his flights to Grenada as soon as he
found out / & having made initial contact it was
time to embark on a colourful noisy voyage to find
his birth father / & in locating him / hopefully / find
out more about his birth mother too

/ / /

he remembers the anticipation / the agony of it /
the queasiness that sat in the pit of his stomach / for
weeks / then on the day of departure / the endless
retching / the need to numb the nerves with drink
/ rum mixed with codeine / travel sickness pills /

anything he could get his hands on really / any
sickly concoction to try to quell the thumping of his
heart / the growing growling ache in his stomach
/ the lead in his legs / the feeling-less thighs as
he stumbled through security towards his gate /
thoroughly frisked by heavy-handed guards in his
quest towards the truth / the journey was turbulent
/ he remembers / not helping settle his already
unsettled stomach / didn't manage to get any sleep
in the eight or so hours it took to get there / & he
felt as lost as ever from the moment he landed /
his light-ish skin marking him out as an outsider /
neither this nor that / somewhere in between / it's
similar back in Belleek / the village straddles the
border / history cuts right through / a line through
the bridge / north vs south / & Aidy straddles a
border of his own / a halfway house / between black
& white / Irish & non-Irish / past & present / from
the moment he stepped off the plane just outside
St Georges there was a swelling strangeness / a
sweltering of something not quite right / hard to
put into words / for a start everything was more

expensive than it needed to be / call it a colour tax /
an untold toll to pay for the lightness of his skin

/ / /

even on a little island / it still took well over an
hour from the airport to reach him / his father
/ find his address / the nerves hurting as he was
dropped by the taxi driver outside the wooden shack
of a house / he was then greeted & ushered inside
by a man in his forties / a relative of Aidy's? / a
brother? / a cousin? / & seconds later there he was
/ unmistakably his father / same face / dark / slim /
fragile & frail / their long-awaited embrace . . . brief

/ / /

Aidy gave it a few days / maybe it was his age / but
despite his best attempts / this man / his dad / who he
was meeting for the first time / remained tight-lipped
about his short stint in England in the fifties / didn't
seem to recall / at all / the moment he met Aidy's

71

birth mother / or very much of what she was like /
or what happened after / he dismissed the past / his
past / with a nonchalant wave / or by simply looking
away / gave a confused look to every question posed
/ despite his silence / Aidy used the few days he had
with him / in the family home / to find out as much
as he could / dig about a bit when the younger man
left for work / or wherever it was he went during the
day / he couldn't help but study & scan every picture
he came across on living room walls / corridors &
hallways / toothy grins of grandchildren / coconut
oil sheen in the hair / & one day / he remembers
stumbling upon a newspaper clipping in one of the
bedrooms at the back of the house / some kind of
advert or something / which read **DR DEATH** in
big bold writing at the top / & this man / his father
/ in his much younger years / sporting a grimacing
wrestling pose ready to pounce / blossoming afro /
donning a garish vest / Aidy's eyes widening as he
read the little bio underneath at speed

Grenadian-born 'Apex' took up wrestling as a hobby to begin with but later decided to make a profession of it. Apex has had two fights. He won one of them and is now waiting to hear from anyone wishing to promote him. His stage name is 'DR DEATH'. Apex is in training all week and if he is not playing in his steel band he trains weekends as well. He also does body building. Apex says wrestling is a worthwhile profession. He would like to see more boys and girls taking it up. For further details on Dr Death contact Albert Promotions

Aidy found it hard to believe as he watched this same man watch the cricket / hard to imagine him having any kind of sporting pedigree / a muscular past / nimbler more physical history / seeming so implausible now looking at him as he sat weak & frail in his chair / cataracted eyes fixed on the screen / unable to mutter just a few useful words about the woman he impregnated back in 1956

*/ / /*

throughout his time on the little island / staying in
the spare room in his father's small house / this man
/ his father / revealed little that Aidy didn't already
know / said he found himself in England for work in
the mid-fifties / just a few months on the docks / *a
passing visit* / he slurred / found it too cold for his
bones / set off again a few months later / if anything
/ he knew as much / or should he say little / about
her / his birth mother / as Aidy did / maybe she
lived in London now / he guessed / *She like England*
/ he said / *Maybe she have another son* / he added
/ *with another man . . . married . . .* / he imagines
/ *maybe she worked at a hospital* / but he wasn't
sure / it was something Aidy had heard before /
none of these rumours were new to him / all just
suggestions & speculation / didn't offer anything
concrete / feelings he may or may not have felt
long forgotten / one day / after quizzing him got
Aidy no nearer the truth / he decided a walk was
needed to clear his head / confronting this old man
& getting nowhere made him feel that this whole
trip had been a waste / a waste of money / a waste

of time / it felt like a defeat / a last-minute missed
penalty / a detective who couldn't crack the case
despite tracking down the number-one witness / he
felt he had failed in his mission to piece his history
together / to make sense of who he was / where he
came from & most importantly / who his mum was
& what she was like / but as he trudged through the
red-mud fields to calm himself down / sun beating
down furnace-hot on his balding head / flip-flop
smacking against his hardened sole / amongst the
guava-laden trees he soon softened / & a few hours
later / he returned to the house / his father's home /
calmer / it wasn't this frail old man's fault he didn't
know the details from all those years ago / couldn't
offer any helpful clue-cracking scraps / it *was* over
fifty years ago / Aidy didn't know whose fault it was
/ but if anything his father was a victim of the times
too / Aidy now knew that this man / his father / had
no idea of his very existence until he received Aidy's
letter / just a couple of months ago

*/ / /*

Aidy resolved it within himself to not get irate anymore / not while there at least / it was clearly too late / his time would be better used to get to know this man before Aidy would inevitably lose him too / so over the next few days on the island Aidy decided to make more of an effort / dig deeper within himself to forgive / build some kind of bond / forge some kind of connection / they discussed Manchester United / even watched a Premier League game together over a couple of beers in the bar just down the road / but even a comfortable win against a relegation-threatened team they should have beaten more convincingly couldn't really bridge the distance between them / even after a week or so he was *still* a stranger to Aidy / & probably always would be / Aidy couldn't imagine himself returning here again / watching the match was the first & only time he saw this man become at all animated / & when the goal went in / the only time on the whole trip he really saw him smile / much earlier than he thought Aidy was ready to go home

on the last day before his flight back / his dad said
he was taking him somewhere / Aidy didn't know
what he was talking about / or where it was he was
going / by now Aidy was keen to finish packing /
keen to get back to Belleek / keen to just forget about
this whole trip / in the ten days Aidy had been on
the island / apart from occasionally walking the few
minutes to the beach / or down to the bar in town /
or circling the fields across the way to clear his head
/ he hadn't really explored anywhere new / his dad
hadn't recommended any sights to see / or offered
to show him different parts of the island or taken
him to visit the rest of his family / even Aidy's half-
brother / who he saw regularly around the house
/ didn't really make the effort to have any kind of
meaningful conversation while he was there / except
once . . . to ask for money / so as Aidy sipped his
cocoa tea that morning he was pretty baffled when
he heard a pick-up truck pull up outside / & his dad
demand some help to get up / first out the house / &

then down the front steps & into this stranger's car /
a spacious five-seater / a man in his forties sat serious
& straight behind the wheel / could have been his
cousin maybe / Aidy wasn't sure / he was driven
for miles / a journey that took over forty minutes
/ right across to the other side of the island / Aidy
had no idea where they were going / the car rocked
side to side / bounced up & down / as they turned off
the main highway onto a much smaller side street
/ diverting off the beaten track / much-changed
terrain / then the driver just stopped / basically in
the middle of the road / in the middle of nowhere /
on this random dirt path / *Here* / the driver said /
coldly / without turning his head / Aidy hopped out
& helped his old dad out of the passenger's side seat
/ his arms all bony & thin / they staggered through
the forest / all thick & dense & green / & after five
minutes or so they reached a little clearing / a gap
in the nature / a natural pause / & as this old man
/ his father / leant against a tree to catch his breath
/ he eventually summoned enough puff to speak /
*This is yours, son* / he said gesturing to the land they

overlooked / *all of it* / Aidy froze / didn't really know
what to say / what to do / how to react / as beautiful
& vast as it was he didn't want it / any of it / all he
wanted was to go home / more than ever now / all
he wanted was to not waste any more time & resume
the search to meet his real mum

/ / /

Aidy's memories of growing up were nothing to
write home about / had no home to actually write to
/ deep down he had no place to call home / not really
/ he remembered always feeling lonely / timid &
scared / treated different to other children / treated
different by other children / all his life feeling like
he's teetering on the edge of something / always on
the cusp / knew from young he was adopted / well
more specifically / put up for adoption / constantly
unsettled by a desire to find the woman who
brought him into this world / to sit down opposite
her / hug her / hold her liver-spotted hands / look
her dead in the face / pinpoint the features of hers

that resemble his / look closely into her eyes / study
the outline of her jawline / the width of her lips /
take it all in / every little bit / breathe *her* in / try
to make sense of what happened / he often thinks
about what she might be doing at any given time /
is she married / does she have other children / listen
to Daniel O'Donnell / have any pets / is she one of
those poor souls who's been waiting two years for
hip surgery? / what radio station does she listen
to? / for years he's trawled through the internet /
scrolled & scrolled / clicked & clicked / spent days /
months / decades / staying up all night just to find
some kind of lead / some hint / some clue / looking
for a something that reveals anything / for years he
has dreamt of reuniting / meeting up somewhere
nice / a restaurant / a nice park / somewhere on the
coast / open up the space to hear her side / her story
/ from her mouth / what exactly happened all those
years ago / how she met his dad / how she actually
feels about giving him up when she did / with Aidy
just eleven months / a baby / but it's been one step
forward two steps back for so many years now /

he thinks / as he joins Osh & Eimear in the Castle
Caldwell car park

*/ / /*

it's only a short drive to Dulrush Lodge / down
the lane / along the gravel path towards the large
guesthouse with the restaurant inside / they park up
/ spot a couple of French fisherman sinking brandies
on one of the picnic benches at the front / toasting
to their earlier catch / trapping trout / pinching pike
/ the temperature is dropping / Eimear wiggles on
her long-sleeve Hollister top as they climb the stairs
towards the entrance of the restaurant perched on
the bank of Lough Erne / Osh still in his t-shirt /
they haven't booked ahead & Aidy is relieved to see
more than enough free seats as they walk in / some
are reserved for later but for now / thankfully /
it's fine / they are immediately greeted by a young
redhead at the door / no more than twenty / looks
sweet / pretty / but Aidy is used to it now / he'll be
seventy soon / being a man of mixed heritage here

in this island of Ireland / half-caste / a half-breed / as he used to be called by many when he was young / he can't not notice *that* little look / the not-so-subtle double-take people do when they see him enter certain spaces / a millisecond of hesitation / so small it's unnoticeable to the untrained eye / but as a man of colour / Aidy knows there's sometimes more to it / it's not just here at Dulrush Lodge / not just here straddling the borderlands of Belleek / & it's not necessarily this young girl's fault / it's just how it is really / & Aidy knows it's worse in other countries / has seen it for himself working all over the world / & that's why he never really complains / not with his mouth anyway / but today / especially with his kids with him / & after what happened yesterday at St Angelo / he's feeling a little more sensitive than usual / of course it's not just here / it could be in the local Spar / or the local library / it's heavy / the burden of being a Black man sometimes / his head hurts / his heart hurts / his hand hurts

/ / /

the three of them follow the flame-haired waitress
to the corner booth & sink into their seats as they
are given their menus / Aidy checks his watch /
knows time is running out to get his story finished
& submitted / feels increasingly uneasy / like he's
letting this opportunity pass him by / he knows
it's going to be tight now / but he can still do it /
he reassures himself / he scribbles more notes on
his phone as Eimear & Osh decide what they want
to eat / at least he thinks he knows what's going
to come next / but won't know for sure until he's
sitting in front of his screen / making a mess with
words / letting himself go / building belief bit by bit
as he edges closer & closer to his target word count
/ doesn't have to be five thousand words exactly /
'up to' the guidelines said / there's flexibility there /
room to play with / Eimear goes for the fish & chips
/ Aidy orders the sea bass / with chips on the side
/ Osh gets both the fish & chips & lasagne with a
sparkling water / he finds it hard but Aidy tries not
to worry about how much this will all come to / tries
hard to be present / live in the moment as much

as he can / enjoy this / it's mad to him how big his
kids have got / so tall & strong / he sneaks a look
at his daughter as she scrolls through her phone &
then a few moments later returns to the book she
was reading yesterday / that Rooney one / she's
making good progress / nearly finished it already
/ she's growing up so quickly / Aidy concedes /
long-limbed / effortlessly athletic / the difference
between her & his now stoutly stature is stark /
although he has always loved sport / he definitely
wasn't as dedicated as her when he was fifteen / even
though his boxing was going well back in the day /
won a few fights / his heart wasn't always in it / yes
he was strong / always able to put on a bit of a show
once in the ring / fancied himself against anyone
on his day / not once was he properly bashed up or
battered blue / but outside of the ring he needed
to be more disciplined if he was going to make a
proper career out of / if he was to make a name for
himself / but boxing to him was more of a thing he
*had* to do to protect himself than something he was
actually *that* invested in / was still living on the

Isle of Man around this time / his foster family had moved there a few years before / & life on the Isle of Man wasn't any easier than what he already had to put up with / there were still the usual sharp-edged stares / comments / gestures / more often than not Aidy was more than capable of brushing them off / took them in his stride most of the time / he had to / but one night / more than a little worse for wear / significantly under the influence / he properly snapped / a late night in his late teens / stumbling home from the boozer / catching up with friends / when someone called him *that* word / & Aidy chased after the racist dickhead / it was pitch black as he sprinted down the high street / clambered over a garden fence / & pummelled him till it hurt to hit anymore / battered him good & proper / a miracle this fella survived really / Aidy's hand today a reminder of the damage he did all those years ago / his knuckles still noticeably deformed / all bent & misshapen / ruled him out of the ring for over half a year at the time / had to have surgery to put his fingers back into place / doctors said he would make a full recovery / but he was never quite the same boxer / had to adjust his style / tinker with his technique / adopt a stance that didn't come naturally / his promising boxing career short-lived basically

/ / /

there's little space left on the table when the food arrives but they manage to manoeuvre enough room to fit it all in / they're all so hungry after their walk they tuck in straight away / moods lifting with every bite / after a few bits of his fish / Aidy sips his lager & feels more than content / he's already half a pint down & it's going straight to his head / in a good way / he's especially enjoying the view of the lake from where they're sat too / at this jovial juncture / & with his pint going down nice / he feels brave enough to ask a question he's been aching to for a while / he's heard the rumours / seen potential evidence on Facebook / *So . . .* / he starts / *. . . have you got a boyfriend then?* / he asks his unsuspecting daughter in the middle of forking a fat chip into her

mouth / Osh looks on amused / whether it's his
dad's boldness or the revealing of a secret he already
knew / Aidy is unsure / Eimear seems a little shy
/ a little annoyed / doesn't really say anything /
nibbling now on the crunchy bits of some fish batter
/ looking a little embarrassed / he already knows
she probably has / saw it on Siobhan's page a few
weeks back / & as much as Aidy knows it was bound
to happen / she's a teenager after all / this silent
confirmation still sits uncomfortably with him /
Aidy moves on / changes subject / *Heard much
from Leo?* / he asks his son / suddenly dreaming
of having all three of his kids together on the
same weekend / he doesn't remember the last time
this has happened / *Not really . . .* / Osh replies
/ nonchalantly / Aidy waits for more / a morsel
/ just a crumb of something / but nothing else is
forthcoming / he looks out onto the view from the
restaurant window / then lets his eyes wander back
inside / a young-ish woman clutching a chicken
wrap catches his eye / one of the other waitresses
on a break / yellow reduced sticker on the wrapper

of her meal deal / animated navy blue Birkenstock
clogs / having coffee & cake with a friend whose
impatient toddler demands an ice cream / high chair
smeared with Ella's Kitchen spag bol / as another
waitress waddles about with a wobbly tray of lattes
/ as he watches life unfold & unravel & reveal itself
around him Aidy returns to thinking about his
story / to thoughts of the mother who's struggling
with it all / trying to pin down whatever it is she's
feeling into some kind of scene that he could write
into his narrative as she navigates this painful limbo
/ struggling under the weight of a grief not yet
fully felt / a breathtaking anguish that affects her
badly but her ex-husband worse / the footballer's
dad / who switches from one extreme to another /
one moment to the next / fury / denial / outrage /
belief / & then loss / time is ticking / Aidy checks
his phone as he gets up for a piss / is confronted
by the usual onslaught of Facebook notifications
as he unlocks his screen / nonsense gaming spam
/ another flurry of messages from Kateryna / she
uses every app she can to contact Aidy / he'll reply

to her later / he will / his hands sting as he washes
them / a reminder of the mess he's made of his fist
/ the clean-up he will have to deal with on Monday
/ he pushes those thoughts to one side for now /
wants to make every minute with his children this
weekend count / *What was better, then?* / Aidy
asks as he returns to the table & sidles back into
the booth / Osh juts his head up / confused / *The
lasagne or the fish and chips?* / Aidy clarifies settling
into the familiar warmth of his seat / *Oh . . .* / he
pauses / *Well . . .* / he says / resetting his knife &
fork into the finished position before scrunching up
his napkin / only the grease from the lasagne left on
either of his plates / *Ah . . . both did a job like* / he
says / *filled a hole . . .* / he adds / the three of them
sit in the silence of their full bellies for a moment /
Aidy gulps down the last of his lager / Eimear scrolls
through her phone / her book open on the table
face down / Osh runs a finger along his bicep before
looking out onto the lake again / Aidy doesn't know
what Osh has planned this evening / if anything
/ but he doesn't want *this* to end / not now / Aidy

looks at his watch / it's still quite early / more than enough time for one / Aidy knows he has a deadline / but for now / you know what? / . . . *Fancy a quick pint at Charlie's?* / Aidy suggests / Osh's not a big drinker / not like others his age / more into his fitness / always has been / tried his hand at every sport since National School / Aidy remembers driving him to hurling / rugby / GAA / & football / has always been keen to keep his body in the best shape / Aidy has never really seen him drink / or smoke / or vape / certainly never seen him drunk / Aidy watches him ponder this suggestion for about a minute / contemplate his options / working out how it might interfere with other plans he might have / despite doing his best to play it cool / not come on too strong / Aidy is sure Osh can read the want in his dad's eyes / the desperation to keep *this* going / have them all together for as long as he can / after a few moments / though maybe not overly keen / it seems / Osh agrees / *One won't hurt, I suppose . . . ain't that right, Lanky* / he says / playfully rubbing the top of her head with the corner of his

fist / Aidy's not a big drinker either / not really / not
one for getting legless on the regular anymore / he's
had more than his fair share of big nights in the past
/ that'll do him / doesn't see the point of drinking
himself silly / squandering his remaining savings on
booze like too many a man around here / down the
Black Cat Cove every day / slouched ugly on the bar
/ spouting nonsense politics over their seventh pint
/ yes he's happy to sink a can or two / now & then /
while writing or watching the news / but that'll do /
he can't handle liquor like he used to

/ / /

the waitress brings over the bill / the meal has
come up to a fair bit but worth every penny /
Aidy concedes as he pays up / cash / then / with
an extra spring in his step / a brisk exit through
the restaurant / filling up nicely now / back down
the stairs & back into the Qashqai / on the other
side / under the glow of an outside heater / a
gaggle of high-spirited hen do-ers / six or seven of

them / disrobe then dip into the bubbling hot tub
before necking their flutes of prosecco / the French
fisherman from before have finished their drinks
/ for now / & have retired for the evening / will
probably be up bright & early again tomorrow /
Aidy imagines / for another day's catch out on the
lake / 'Up De Flats' starts to play automatically as
Aidy pulls out of the car park / drives back up the
lane & along the gravel path / turns right along Boa
Island Road towards Enniskillen / & Charlie's / not
left towards Belleek / & home

/ / /

he didn't sleep that much last night & tiredness is
creeping in driving along the same road he usually
takes to work / thoughts of yesterday's altercation
resurface / the mess he's made / of the situation /
of his hand / hasn't dared check his work emails /
he's archived the work WhatsApp group chat / as
he drives he rubs his index finger along the abrasive
skin where the wound struggles to heal / right in

the bony bend of the knuckle / perhaps he shouldn't
have lost his temper like he did / especially in front
of customers / but he was asking for it / this new
chef half Aidy's age / showed no respect / even
though Aidy has worked there for well over ten
years / much longer than this guy has been in the
country / probably / has no right to be talked to
that way / called *that* word in front of a café full
of people / most of his time at St Angelo / as the
airport is still known to many / has been good /
rewarding even / has certainly kept him busy when
he needed to be following his divorce from Siobhan
/ more or less left to his own devices / which he
likes / . . . liked / & over the years / he has seen this
little airfield grow / was only built during the second
world war / used for commercial flights long before
his time / but the council took it over after 9/11 &
the little airport started to struggle / in theory you
could fly to Cancun / in reality to England at best
/ but things have been picking up again in recent
years & it can actually get quite busy sometimes
/ overseeing the day-to-day running of things /

keeping it all in order / passenger numbers going up
& up / hence the recent reopening of the old café /
turning it into a much fancier new diner / hence the
need for a new chef / Aidy's specific role is hard to
explain / an 'odd jobs' man you could say / helping
out with everything from clearing any debris on
the tarmac to fixing broken fences / everything &
anything that needs doing really / would be a shame
to leave all that behind for some racist who took
offence at Aidy's perfectly reasonable request that
he shouldn't be vaping out at the front as customers
were walking in / he got defensive at first / then
angry / spoiling for a fight he was / shouting &
pointing & swearing / regretted that when he was
knocked out cold with a single punch / Aidy's fist
/ his face / smack / Aidy stayed at the scene long
enough to see him groggily get back to his feet /
ensure he hadn't caused any lasting damage / won't
know for sure till Monday though

/ / /

thirty minutes or so after leaving Dulrush Lodge the
three of them arrive into the centre of Enniskillen /
Ireland's only island town / Aidy parks by the
Buttermarket / he knows he won't have to pay / so
late in the day / traffic wardens will have clocked off
/ they wander the long way round / dander down
the high street / past old banks / old hotels /
churches / town halls / Sports Direct / closed-down
Topman / *'Now we're sucking diesel'* / the mural
reads / *Line of Duty* star Adrian Dunbar was born
round here / still loved round these parts / as
expected / Charlie's is busy as they enter / but not
yet entirely full / flat-screen TVs blare bright green
/ reflect off bald patches / showing highlights on
mute from this week's matches in the Premier
League / Christy Moore singing through the
speakers / framed rugby shirts on the wall / football
scarves strung up like bunting on the ceiling /
United / Chelsea / Liverpool / Osh & Eimear shuffle
straight to one of the only free booths / perfectly
positioned just yards from the bar / ushered on
hurriedly by Aidy / keen to nab the seats quickly

before they are taken / before he has to lift his head up properly & confront more subtle double-takes than he's already experienced today / Aidy knows this place will be rammed later / the early-evening atmosphere already bubbling / brewing / laughter & conversation about sport & Stormont & the cost of living & family black sheep spending their last few pennies on drink heard in haughty snippets just above the hubbub of musicians setting up in the raised seating area in the corner / a guitar strum / a beat of the bodhrán / a finger of the fiddle / the banjo player has a puff of his vape / a stool is moved / moved again / at the bar Aidy spots a slice of hairy arse-crack / a straining Primark belt just about hanging on / tattoo sleeves snaking up to necks / a Celtic cross & a couple of Claddaghs / scuffed Slazengers / a drunk woman complaining about how Enniskillen has gone to shit / how the whole island of Ireland has gone to shit / & moments later / randomly / how she wouldn't eat anything celeb chef James Martin cooked even if you paid her / before shuffling out to the Ladbrokes next door to

put a bet on / half a lager left at the bar to come back
to later / staff continue jovially pint-pulling /
checking in with the regulars / questioning the plans
of the newbies / letting the Guinness goodness settle
/ rest / then fizz to a foam like marshmallow at the
top / bulbous & bulging / there's a couple of lads /
six or seven / wearing Fermanagh shirts / ill-fitting
bootcuts / slip-on square-toe loafers / roaring in the
corner / madhouse pissed / full-throated chanting /
rebel-song loud like they're at Croke Park & it's cup
final day / skin-tight jerseys strangling throbbing
veins / glinting knock-off watches catching the
strobe light / Eimear has been taken here before /
many times / but seems a little unsure about the
intensity of this booze-fuelled Saturday-night
energy / but once she sits down / has a moment or
two to take in the warmth of this increasingly lively
atmosphere / she soon eases into it / relaxes / Aidy
goes up to order / Guinness / Rockshore / & a Coke
for Eimear / paid for in cash / of course / as the
barman lets the Guinness settle / Aidy surveys the
scene / scans & studies it / sees women dressed to go

'out out' in tall tall heels necking colourless shots /
as lovely as they look / as beautiful as they seem / as
friendly as they might be / he wouldn't dare
approach / wouldn't dare say 'hello' / not brave
enough these days / just happy now to admire from
afar / silently / but still feels a pang of something
deep down / checks his phone as the barman fills his
glass to the top / another message from Kateryna /
doesn't open it / yet / she never *not* messages / he
doesn't have to look at it to know there will be a
flurry of love hearts / kisses / & improbably perfect
pictures of her half-naked / in bed / pre-workout /
post-workout / she's always desperate to get in
touch / interact / & he's told her already that he's
with his kids this weekend but she's credit-card keen
/ horny for him apparently / her words / & Putin is
unrelenting & she says she's been crying every day
since the conflict began & she's feeling isolated &
lonely & Aidy is war-torn about whether to open it /
open up / whether to reply / whether to part with
his money / again / what he's been paying for
exactly in recent weeks is unclear / but despite

costing him an arm & a leg it's been doing the job of
keeping some of the loneliness away / temporarily
at times at least / he puts his phone back in his
pocket & with his right hand still sore clutches the
three drinks tight as he makes his way back to his
kids in the booth & settles himself in / after each sip
Aidy finds himself studying the contents more
closely / appreciating the frothy beauty of the
creamy residue / letting it linger for longer on his
lips / then his tongue / marvelling at whatever
magic it is that makes it so damn moreish / Charlie's
is properly rammed now / more & more voices
joining in with the band's jaunty singing / everyone
seems to know all the words of the current song /
people coming in for *just the one* an hour or so ago
have strapped in for the long run / have properly
found their voice / Aidy doesn't sing along / yet /
but hums to the semi-familiar melodies even though
he doesn't exactly know all the lyrics / strobe lights
flash green / flash pink / flash blue / more Guinness
is consumed / Eimear hasn't checked her phone for
at least fifteen minutes / or taken out her book /

right here / right now / the energy in this place is
more than entertainment enough / the three of
them tap their feet to the beat / Aidy is drumming
along with his fingers / the little wooden table sticky
with a concoction of liquids / lager / stout / sugar /
Osh gets another round in & Aidy praises his
forward-thinking / even though he's not yet
eighteen technically no-one bats an eyelid around
here / no-one minds / no-one cares / *That's my boy!*
/ he shouts / as he downs the last drop & slams his
glass back down ready for the one Osh will bring /
the Guinness still tasting as delicious as it was a few
hours ago / through the crowd Aidy can see his son
/ bopping his head & drumming to the beat at the
bar / pulling trigger fingers as if the Irish music the
band play is a song by Dave or Central Cee or
Stormzy / Aidy hasn't really thought this through
as he downs it in one / he's definitely had too many
to drive home now / even round here / he's lost
count of how many he's had / but he'll worry about
that later / that last pint tasted as good as the first so
he signals to the busy barman to pour him another /

& he obliges / winking back at Aidy knowingly / as
the band finish their song & the growing crowd of
pint-drinkers & spirit-sippers & foot-tappers & hip-
shakers show their appreciation with a hearty
applause / they restart with a song that Aidy doesn't
recognise as well as the Irish ones from before /
doesn't matter though / because right now his head
is swelling with a long-unfelt joy / swirling with a
pleasure that's been a long time coming / his head's
beginning to spin / thinking about Eimear & Osh &
Leo somewhere & being here & Kateryna & the
short story competition & maybe fucking winning it
& making something of himself for once & maybe
then his real mum might sit up & take notice /
recognise his name & want to see him / acknowledge
he exists / there are no free seats for the newbies
who enter / clip-clopping & tip-toeing in their open-
toed 'going out out' high heels / it's standing room
only now / a group of women wiggle their hips to
the fiddler's fizzing fingers right by Aidy's table /
their dresses at risk of getting wet / as one song ends
/ the band transition into another / begin playing

renditions of modern hits that Aidy isn't that familiar with / in seconds of this new song starting / Eimear's smile extends into full-beam / wide eyes headlight-bright / it's clearly a song she knows / a song she likes / Aidy has sunk five six pints / maybe seven / maybe more / he isn't sure / lost count long ago / but Eimear is drunk on the sugar of her Coke & the sheer joy of the music playing & the legless liveliness of this moment / as the band play / tapping their feet to their own beat / more & more people get up from their seats / to the right / a young girl / early twenties / in a little black dress has mounted the table & is re-enacting Michael Flatley's *Riverdance* / Aidy's eyes pop / shocked / the barmen have stopped pouring to look & start clapping / Guinness foam slides down their hairy forearms as they applaud the impressive performer / *Come on, Dad, let's dance!* / Aidy is taken aback by this out-of-the-blue suggestion / he's no dancer / *You must know this one?* / she says / even if Aidy was sober he's not sure he would have a clue / *It's Ed Sheeran, Dad!* / she shouts delighted / swishing her long curly hair side to side to the beginning of the song / Aidy has heard of Ed Sheeran / obviously / but doesn't know this one / *Oh my God, Dad, it's 'Galway Girl'! Come on!* / Aidy is hoisted to his feet by his daughter's strong arms / her hockey-hardened biceps / she directs him towards the tiny dancefloor / though too drunk to really appreciate it / he tries to savour every second of her touch / palm on palm / as they slalom through the blur of bodies to the packed dancefloor to get closer to the band / Aidy is squashed / sandwiched in between fleshy necks & armpit sweat / pinned down by pure joy / they've made it into the middle / & he's suddenly right in the thick of it / basking in the delight of others chanting the lyrics of a song Aidy barely knows / riotous renditions of a song he's unsure he's ever heard before / he feels as drunk as he has for years / he feels the youngest he has for years / he wants to twirl his daughter like a *Strictly* contestant / so he does / & she lets him / & they bump into others / but it doesn't matter / no-one minds / *This is a tuuuuune, Dad!* / she shouts / she's now

twirling him / & he spins / one spin feels like three /
then out of nowhere / Osh re-appears / has entered
the fray with more drinks / joins in with the jigging
& jiving / & his re-emergence is met with the
reaction of that of a long-lost friend they haven't
seen for years / they cheers & clink their glasses /
causing extra spillage to the already sticky
dancefloor / but it's too busy for anyone to care / too
rammed for anyone to notice / they are all together
/ three bodies / swaying to the music as one / a song
that Aidy didn't know a few minutes ago is now
probably his favourite song ever / he twerks &
whines / jiggles & jives / it's been ages since he's felt
this alive / a stranger's hand clutches his / & Aidy
recoils at first / has he been too naïve? / let his guard
down? / allowed for a lapse of concentration / drawn
the attention of a troublemaker / but as he looks
down he clocks it's just the manicured-nailed hand
of an innocent woman who wants to dance / could
be one of the fancy dressers from before maybe /
eyes are disco-ball big / Aidy downs the rest of his
pint / they wiggle & twist / twirl & spin / everyone

is clapping / everything is spinning now / around & around / it's all suddenly too much / he thinks he's going to fall down / *I've got a girlfriend!* / he tries to get out / shout / he's fisheye-lens drunk staggering away from the dancefloor now / somehow / swimming in the deep end / needs a breather / a timeout / a sit-down somewhere / he's stumbling / bumping into people / feels a hand or two on his shoulder / someone calling his name / there's a dangle of keys & suddenly Aidy feels toe-tippy light on his feet / like he's being carried / strong-armed / swept away somewhere / he feels the muscle of a man / a voice in his ear / the music going from too loud to just right / then quieter & quieter until he can't hear it at all anymore / but can soon feel the coolness of outside / *Good lad, Osh, good lad . . .* / Aidy slurs / seeing the shape of his son's face through the blur / & Eimear too? / *Is that you, love?* / feeling the cold air on his gut / then the warmer inside of a car / doors slamming shut / all that Guinness bubbling & brewing in his belly / stewing in his stomach / & slowly rising / feels it

fleshy in his throat / . . . *Did I tell you both? . . .* / he
spits out / words all slurred / *I've been writing this*
*new story*

# SUNDAY

# THE ACHE TAKES STRANGLEHOLD / GUT-PUNCH

throbs / heartbeat fast from throat to fist & down
to his feet / a pulse-pounding pain so sharp it pin-
prick stings / throat clenched-fist closed / stomach
heavy / groaning foghorn loud / achingly unhappy
/ fucking hell / fuck me! / he thinks / *What the fuck
happened last night?* / Aidy mumbles / blinking
himself awake / suddenly shooting up in his bed &
flinging off his duvet / sees he's wearing the same
clothes he was all of yesterday / feels all battered &
bruised / unsteady & fragile / sluggish & confused
/ checks the time on his phone / it's black-screen
dead / *Ah fuck!* / he says / starting to retrace his
steps / starts with what he does remember / Castle
Caldwell / yes / Dulrush Lodge / yes / Charlie's /
yes / sort of / Guinness / more Guinness / woman
at the bar shouting about James Martin / pint after

pint / music he knew turning into songs he didn't
/ then it really starts to blur / strobe-light bright /
too much Guinness / he doesn't remember how he
/ how they? / got home / & where are they now? /
Osh & Eimear / *Fuck!* / he stumbles to his feet jelly-
legged & weak / the headrush hurts like a blow to
the head / he stumbles over to the window / prises
the slats of the blinds open with two shaking fingers
/ is more than relieved to see his car in the drive /
seemingly unscathed / still very much intact / but
he doesn't know how it's got there & he's suddenly
terrified / did he drive home drunk? / where's Osh
/ where's Eimear? / he makes for the door / head
spinning / room spinning / leaning on the edge of
the bed for support / wallpaper all red & white / he's
about to shout his children's names but then / to
his relief / as he swings open his bedroom door he
spots their trainers / Eimear's all-white Air Forces &
Leo's all-black New Balances / strewn on the top of
the landing / they must have bunked up together in
the spare room for the night / he's relieved but his
heart's still going as he races to the toilet to be sick /

followed by a much-needed shit / sitting / straining / shifting / struggling to wipe himself clean / in this state Aidy knows it's touch & go whether he'll make the deadline now / still has to write the third & final part of his story / knows the clock is ticking / hopes there'll be enough time to squeeze in some kind of ending but that feels far off right now / has no plans to go to church this morning / never does anyway / & United are playing later / desperately needs a coffee / to wash away the taste lingering on the tip of his tongue / he shuffles downstairs / thinks about firing up the Nespresso machine but is worried the whirling might wake Eimear & Osh / opts for instant instead / back-of-the-cupboard Kenco / he fills the kettle up & clicks it on / hunching over the sink as it boils bright blue / trying to compose himself / get it together / snap himself out of this fucking mess / his laptop open / ready & raring to go / he staggers towards it / his head hurts / a lot / but he really must get on with finishing what he has started / looks at his oversized wall-mounted clock with thick black hands / will be a job to get it done now he knows /

but as he logs in & checks the number at the bottom
left-hand corner / he realises he's actually somehow
written more than he thought

/ / /

now / somehow / he's just under a thousand words
short of his target of five thousand / he speed reads
the last few pages of the Word doc / it's a sort of
rambling stream-of-consciousness / this third &
final section of his short story / 'About to Fall Apart'
/ is told in third person / his eyes fizz down the page
/ there aren't any full stops / it's just one winding
sentence / creative reflections about life & death /
despite the state he was in last night / as he reads
/ it seems he's produced something he's sort of
proud of / he writes a new line / spells something
wrong deliberately to check if Word is still working
/ check he can still actually string sentences together
containing words that actually exist / he can /
feels like he's building something slowly / he's
agonisingly close to the revelation that just three

months after the death of her son in the backseat
of a no-good plane that nosedived into the water
/ metal slamming thunderously into the sea / the
devastating news / kicking her when she was already
down / that her son's dad / her ex-husband / flew
his wings too / yep / the pair of them / father & son
dead / the cause of his untimely demise / a broken
heart / just like that / gone & gone / in less than a
year / three becoming one / their quest for answers
/ for justice / his grief / ultimately / the perpetrator
/ in too quick of a time to compute / take in fully /
this woman on her knees already / daily / has lost
the two main men in her life / she feels doubly dead
now / somehow / she has no-one to do nothing with
/ is struggling / expects to die herself soon / wants
to die herself soon / join them wherever they are /
every day she tries to navigate the perpetual pain
that pounds away at her / entwines around her /
entraps her / has its dirty mitts around her throat /
grabbing & squeezing / gasping & wheezing / ready
to strangle her / throttle her to death / ready to
swallow her up whole

in the quiet moments / in bed unable to sleep /
cooking / cleaning / in the silence of the toilet /
she wonders about them / wonders if they are
above her / with her / in her? / then all of a sudden
Aidy is startled by Osh who says he's *starrrrving*
breezily entering the kitchen grabbing a Man
United-branded pint glass from the draining board
& pouring himself a full pint of water / in his tight
white t-shirt / GAA shorts / *And me!* / Eimear
shouts from upstairs / Aidy nods soberly / agrees
a good breakfast is needed / desperately / *What a
drunken fool I am . . .* / he says / turning around
in his seat to face his son directly / embarrassed
about not remembering much about last night /
*I'm completely stumped, son . . . and to be honest
. . . scared to ask . . . but not a clue how we got back
last night* / Osh gulps down half of his first glass
in one & refills it to the top / *I drove us* / he says
/ taking another sip / *Even pissed you aren't half
the backseat driver . . . 'Speed up, slow down, left*

*here, right there,'* a human satnav . . . *Eimear will*
*tell ya* / Aidy gulps hard / *He's right!* / she shouts
/ voice muffled / fluoride-full / halfway through
brushing her teeth / Aidy is mortified / Osh has a
licence / was fortunately added to Aidy's insurance
recently / *Were you not over the limit?* / Aidy asks
amazed they made it back in one piece / *Nah, only*
*had a few, was on the Lucky Saints mainly* / lucky
saint indeed / a soundless beat / *Thanks, son, got*
*myself into a right state, didn't I?* / Aidy replies /
relieved / desperate now to give his son a hug but
knowing that mightn't go down that well / stays
rooted to his seat instead / *No bother, we couldn't*
*sleep in Charlie's, could we?* / Aidy still aches all
over / feels tarmac flat / dizzy / existing on empty
/ *What are you thinking for breakfast then?* / he
asks / *Not much in but we could go to Tête-à-Tête. . .*
*or Shannon's?* / these days Aidy's never sure he's
ever suggesting the right things to his children / &
to be honest / the idea of breakfast in Ballyshannon
fills him with dread a little bit / there's too much
history there / Siobhan etc. / *Or there's lots of*

*places in Bundoran we could try . . . I hear Foam*
*is good* / again he feels out of touch / past his sell-
by date / not confident in himself / not sure of the
validity of his words / *I think Leo's working at The*
*Toastery today . . . It's decent in there actually* /
Osh proclaims / washing up his glass before putting
it back upside down on the dingy dishcloth / Aidy
didn't know his son was working there / doesn't
know where *there* is / has never heard of The
Toastery / but it doesn't matter / he can't remember
the last time he's had *all* his kids together / in
the same place / enjoying each other's company /
breathing the same air / eating & drinking / chatting
& joking / joshing & jibing / taking the piss out of
each other / all that normal stuff siblings should
do / he's almost salivating at the prospect of it / so
lost in this image he hasn't even answered Osh yet
/ who waits for a response / confused by his dad's
hesitation / *Sounds perfect, son* / perfect

/ / /

he heard somewhere / said by someone he can't
remember / that you should always finish a writing
session in the middle of writing a new line / a little
trick to maintain the momentum next time you
open the story up / helps get the brain engaged
right away / so mid-sentence he presses save / slams
his laptop shut / & shuffles upstairs to shower in
desperate need to scrub himself clean

/ / /

it takes Aidy longer than it should to feel cleansed
/ he lets the water wash over him for longer than
usual / drenches himself in it / lathering himself
with Original Source / the green one that hurts /
the minty one that stings / & scrubs his skin hard
/ over & over / he almost immediately feels better
than he did / but still no more than half a human
/ needs food / desperately / a spice bag & gravy / a
chicken fillet roll / a full Irish / a full English / eggs
Benedict / pancakes / granola & yoghurt / cod liver
oil & the orange juice / anything & everything / he

gets dressed quickly / spurred on by the growing
growling ache in his tummy / staggers down the
stairs / Osh & Eimear are ready already / slouched
on the sofa / scrolling & pinching at their phone
screens until Aidy ushers them up & outside /
the three of them clamber into the Qashqai / they
trundle back towards Enniskillen with the urgency
of their hunger being as pressing as a medical
emergency / Aidy's head is spinning propeller-fast
/ feels all fidgety / shaky & sick / shuttling down
Lough Shore Road / concentrating hard on reacting
quickly enough / if needed to / it was on this same
stretch a few months ago he crashed / so these days
he's extra careful / was driving Eimear to a dentist
appointment that afternoon / to the practice just
before the hospital when some idiot pulled out
from a side road / Aidy reacted as quickly as he
could but avoiding it was impossible / impact was
inevitable / not enough road to brake in time / he
was going under the speed limit mind / but still
fast enough to cause sufficient damage / he still
remembers the bang / the bone-shaking clang of

the two cars coming together / the car / his car / a
complete write-off / Eimear was fine / thank God /
& so was Aidy really / just a really sore shoulder /
despite it being the early afternoon / turns out the
other driver was steaming drunk / well over the
limit / not a great surprise around these parts / &
now / as he drives down this same road desperate
for a distraction / he thinks about lines for his
story / trying to retain fragments of ideas he'd like
to add / he knows time is running out but despite
the hangover / & the hunger / & the impending
deadline / he feels more content now than he
has in a while / the kids / his kids / chat amongst
themselves / about what exactly / Aidy isn't sure
/ both of them in the privileged condition of not
feeling as rough as he does this morning / they can
comfortably string sensible-sounding sentences
together / maintain a proper conversation / Eimear
has taken charge of the music / & to Aidy's surprise
he recognises the song as soon as it starts / harp-
heavy / a fast funky beat / modern / pop-y / boppy /
*Who's this then?* / Aidy dares to ask / syllables still a

little slurred / in his rear-view mirror he sees Eimear laughing / *Getting forgetful in your old age eh, Da?* / Osh chips in then / *It's the same song from yesterday . . . 'Up De Flats', Gemma Dunleavy* / he says / playfully poking Aidy's temple before turning the music up for them all to sing along to the now familiar chorus

*/ / /*

to the best of his ability in his current state & using all his experience / Aidy parallel parks into a free space conveniently close to the entrance of The Toastery just as another car pulls out / they clamber out of the Qashqai & bundle straight inside / it's busy / pretty much full / noisy with the clang of cutlery / the scraping of plates / the slurping of soup spoons & general congregative Sunday-morning chatter / but despite their collective hunger / no-one comes to greet them initially as they wait to be served / seated / fed / replenished / Aidy spots Leo more or less straight away / his big son / oldest of three / behind the counter / with his back turned to them / pinstriped blue apron & matching hat / about to carefully plate up something delicious / Leo's been good with his hands since his younger days / Play-Doh / Lego / PVA glue / papier-mâché / has always loved his food too / so working in a kitchen makes complete sense / Aidy isn't entirely sure but from the little Osh said he thinks this job here is temporary / but from here he looks at ease / more than competent / confident even / Aidy feels all fizzy with pride / as they wait / Leo glances back briefly & spots them & gives a little nod

/ / /

after a few moments a table for four becomes free & they are shown to their seats by one of the friendly waiters / Leo gives them a little wave with a latex-gloved hand / offers a hint of a smile / now seated & keen to keep the order simple they all order the same thing / recommended to them by the waiter / the chicken & cheese toastie with the carrot &

coriander soup / side of coleslaw / glancing around
Aidy notices the portions look generous / he doubts
Eimear will manage it all / she barely made a dent
with the fish & chips at Dulrush yesterday / but as
much as he wants to say something / he bites his
tongue / is tempted to ask the waiter whether he'll
get a discount since his son works here / but keeps
quiet for now / he reminds himself to just enjoy
moments like these / no fussing / no fretting

/ / /

stomach / & head / still creaky-floorboard fragile /
Aidy has ordered all the liquids / apple juice / coffee
/ Coke / sparkling water / attempts to flush out the
system with a bit of everything / before taking out
his phone & wading through more explicit messages
from Kateryna / slyly angling it away from the
innocent eyes of his children / airbrushed pictures
of her half-naked / he *should* feel turned on / but
really he just wants to know if she's real / if she's
safe? / he would pay double what he does every

other day just to actually meet her / ask her / with
all that's going on over there / whether she would
like a hug? / he imagines her flying to Ireland &
picking her up from the airport / the real miracle of
Knock / he imagines a future / holidays / marriage
/ kids? / the waiter arrives then / & as he serves
the food / there's no waiting / they all get stuck
straight in / crunching into their toasties / slurping
their soup with relish / savouring every morsel of
the coleslaw / this place might not have been an
obvious choice but the food is going down well /
each delicious mouthful filling a hole / the salt / the
fat / the sugar / the holy trinity / it's now less busy
than when they first arrived / less noisy now too /
so as they tuck in / comment on the high quality
of the food in between each satisfying mouthful /
they can actually hear each other properly / there's
sometimes an occasional silence & Aidy is desperate
to fill the void with something / but potential
conversation starters seem to get stuck in his throat
/ lodged stiff / doesn't feel like he has anything
meaningful to say / not while still in this semi-

human state anyway / so stays quiet instead / & just
sits back & observes / Aidy doesn't know how long
this place has been open for but would already be
happy to come back

/ / /

there's a long enough lull in customers for Leo to
whisper something in his manager's ear / Aidy
spots / watching his oldest son untie his apron
straps & bound it over to their table / a mixture
of excitement & joy surges through Aidy as Leo
gets closer & closer / *I'm slaving it back there and
yous are stuffing your faces full, are ya?* / he says
/ giving Eimear a little peck on the top of her head
& pouring himself a glass of water from the jug /
*Hello son, how you keeping?* / Aidy asks / rising
from his seat to give him a hug / Leo hesitates /
seemingly inconvenienced about having to get up
again having sat down / or just embarrassed / Aidy
isn't sure / *Yous looked rough coming in, late one,
was it?* / he asks / accepting the embrace quickly

before finding his seat again / *Especially you, Da
...* / he says / before gulping down his water / &
then applying a generous splodge of handcream
into his palm & beginning to moisturise his fingers
/ *You could say that, son* / Aidy replies sheepishly
/ they soon start chatting about what they got up
to yesterday / Eimear & Osh chipping in now &
then to paint a clearer picture of what happened in
Charlie's specifically / dancing to Ed Sheeran & stuff
/ after a while Aidy sits back / lets them bond / lets
them bicker / he knows they occasionally meet up
without him / but also knows it's not often enough
/ *How's work been, Dad?* / Leo asks out of the blue
/ after all that's gone on this weekend / Aidy had
temporarily forgotten all about work / what he did
on Friday afternoon / & what might happen when
he goes in tomorrow / if he still even has a job to
go to / there will be looks / messages & meetings
/ a possible disciplinary / or a straight-up sacking
on the spot / depends on how hard he hit him / he
thinks / depends on how fierce he defends himself /
depends on how much he cares / maybe he should

just quit anyway / he thinks / get in there first / he's been considering packing it in for a while anyway / & who knows / maybe this writing thing might take off / *Yeah, good, son, not much to report really* / he replies / lies / throat dry / water jug in need of a refill / *This place is nice, son, never been before, you happy here?* / him & his eldest son chat / about work / about contracts / holiday pay / about Man United / & the game against Arsenal starting in a bit / Super Sunday / the others join in & Aidy eases back / lets the scene sink in / takes this moment to think about his story / the final section of the three / the mother still coming to terms / the trying to at least / with what happened in section one / the death of her son / how life has just gone on / *What time do you finish?* / Aidy asks / Leo sips more of his water / *I'm done for the day, only helping out, colleague's ill* / after months of dreaming of moments like now / *this* should be more than enough / ten fifteen minutes altogether / but he tries his luck anyway / *Fancy a lift home?* / Aidy offers / stomach tight / there's a pause like a slow pulse / Leo *can* drive but chooses

not to / *Yeah alright, ta, Da* / his relationship with
Leo has always been up & down but especially of late
/ Aidy would admit he's still adjusting to it / him /
his son coming out / Aidy didn't take it as well as
Leo hoped when he introduced him to Ben for the
first time last Christmas even though all the signs
had been there for years / he's of a different time /
it just wouldn't fly back in his day / he knows things
are different now / Ireland is changing / changed / &
he knows he's falling behind / *Give me two minutes
. . .* / Leo says / getting up & heading back behind
the counter to speak to his boss briefly / Aidy downs
the rest of his Coke / softening ice cubes rattling
in the glass / pays / cash / & waits for his son to
return before heading back out / the four of them /
climbing into the Qashqai / he can see each of their
mums in each of their faces / he uses the second or
two it takes to switch the engine on to take it in / his
three children sharing the same space / breathing the
same air / joking & laughing / Aidy is frozen / the
magic of the moment leaving him stationary / he has
dreamt of days like this for years / perhaps without

the hangover / but the food has helped / gone down well / & even with his deadline / right here / right now / he's full-stomach happy / *We gonna get going, Dad?* / Leo asks / looking at him squarely / clearly wondering what the hold-up is / *Yes, son, sorry . . . let's hit the road*

/ / /

he now has three separate stops to make but Aidy doesn't mind / how could he? / they're all content on their phones as he pulls out & heads back towards the border / Leo in the passenger's seat watches the match / has tilted his screen landscape on his lap / Osh & Eimear share a screen at the back & watch too / the sounds of the match that has just kicked off / the cheers & groans / whistles & commentator curses / all a reminder of his story he has to finish about his dead footballer whose body has been brought back home / the mother's grief felt so real now it lives / breathes / follows / stalks / goes where she goes / exists where she doesn't

/ / /

the border has been crossed / as United start
strong / grow into the game / Aidy drives through
Ballyshannon / past Dorrians to his left / past
Shannon's Corner to his right / up the N15 /
he's going in order / dropping Eimear off first /
in Creevy / then Osh / up near Coolmore / then
Leo / in Cavangarden / 'Up De Flats' has become
the soundtrack of the weekend / & when the song
slows to its end / Aidy instinctively starts it from
the beginning again / it just plays & plays until he
reaches stop one of three ten minutes or so later /
turning into the drive of the house he & Siobhan
once shared / built together / in fact / from scratch
/ project managed brick by brick / & being here
again erupts something in him / a simmering of
something / a tightness / bubbling / deep inside /
a retching regret / he braces himself / attempts to
pre-empt an awkward goodbye with his daughter /
potentially another awkward hello with his ex-wife /
gets in early with the former / *When's that game of*

*yours again, love?* / Aidy asks / as cheerfully as he
can muster / beginning to open his driver's side door
/ preparing to get out / inhale the fresh air needed to
breathe / *Next Thursday . . . playing the team that's
top of the league* / she says / untangling her feet
from the straps of her rucksack / one eye still on the
game on Osh's phone as she opens the door / Aidy
might be far from the best dad in Donegal / but he's
proud to have raised three United fans at least / *I'll
be there* / Aidy says / & after a short pause / *Always*
/ he adds / Aidy has gone to quite a few of Eimear's
matches before but has never seen her eyes light
up quite this bright / maybe something is shifting
/ *You don't have to, Dad* / she says / wanting him
to / clearly / *I'll see you there, sweetheart* / he says
defiantly / *Yeah, I'll try and make it down too* / Osh
chips in without looking up from the match / the
referee has just waved away a United penalty appeal
/ Aidy sees / catching a glimpse of Leo's screen in
the front seat / VAR are not even having a look /
*Yeah, why not* / he adds / immersed in the glow of
the phone / & as all three are just about to agree on

a meeting place next week / another car suddenly
pulls into the driveway / a bright yellow VW Polo
/ unapologetically garish / immodestly modified
/ a souped-up boy racer basically / whizzing in
& skidding to a sharp stop / Aidy can't quite see
the figure inside through the tinted windows /
but knows exactly who he is / what he looks like /
Aidy gets out / waiting for his daughter to say her
goodbyes to Osh on one side / & then Leo on the
other / tries to see through the windscreen of the
yellow Polo / whoever's inside seems oblivious to his
stare / the green glow of a phone reflecting on his
face suggesting he's probably watching the football
too / *So . . . I'll see you on Thursday, princess* / in
the upstairs window / Aidy spots a dressing-gowned
figure / the unmistakable shape of Siobhan / joined
moments later by the more muscular silhouette of
Darragh / in his dressing gown too / both briefly
looking down at what's going on before embracing
each other & turning away / Aidy pauses as Eimear
says the rest of her goodbyes & skips towards the
driver coming out of the yellow car / he stays to see

his daughter & this boy kiss / which literally makes
his toes curl / on spotting Aidy looking at him the
boy gives him a thumbs up / & at this perfectly
innocent gesture Aidy takes a deep breath to stop
feeling dizzy / waves back / & gets back into his car
quickly / both the boys spot him too then / Eimear's
'friend' / give him a thumbs up / a genuine one /
like they've met before / then casually continue
watching the football on their screens / Arsenal have
scored / United are losing / again / not knowing
what to make of it / what to do with himself / his
ex-wife & her new fella / this boy in the yellow Polo
/ he checks his mirrors & slowly U-turns away out
the drive trying not to look back

/ / /

his next stop is Osh / & he's expecting another
frosty reception from Celeste / *When's your*
*next run, son?* / Aidy asks his younger son who's
engrossed in the match still sat at the back / United
sound under the cosh but hoping to not concede

another & let the game get completely out of reach
/ but Aidy's feeling like he's on a roll here / inching
closer to his children turn by turn / one stop at a
time / at a steady speed he drives past the new-
build bungalows set back from the main road / past
the barns / past the fields / hay bales & grazing
cattle / *I'm doing . . .* / Osh pauses as United miss a
really good chance on the counter against the run
of play / a proper sitter it sounds like judging by
Gary Neville's groans / *. . . a half-marathon end of
August . . . up in Letterkenny* / how long's a half-
marathon in miles / Aidy wonders / he considers
it for a minute / savours the image of father & son
limbering up at the start line / the both of them
stretching & warming up before the gun goes off
/ running side by side / stride by stride / initially
/ but then / eventually / setting him free / letting
him go / allowing him to run on & on further into
the distance / could Aidy *really* do it with his dodgy
knee? / & just the one good shoulder / in reality /
probably not / *What date's that, then?* / Aidy could
at least go & support or something / drive up early

/ or book a hotel room the night before maybe /
a Raddison Blu / have a proper day out / it's been
years since he's been up to Letterkenny / could go
for lunch somewhere afterwards / how long would
he take to finish? / Aidy wonders / pausing / *I'll put
it in my diary* / Aidy says / eyes focused hard on the
road ahead / Osh looks for something to say / thinks
about replying but then goes back to the match / Leo
is watching it too but doesn't seem as engrossed now
as Osh at the back / especially as United are losing /
instead / with the phone lying limp in his hand / Leo
looks out of the window in long spells / the weather
/ all things considered / has been good this weekend
& he seems to be taking it all in / deeply / all the
colours of the landscape / like it's the last time he'll
ever see another nice Donegal afternoon

/ / /

round here the weather can be deceiving / even
when the sun's out it's freezing / trees leaning
a little to the left for their life / but for now it's

actually / surprisingly / nice / understandably he's
been more careful behind the wheel since the crash
a few months back / & although he wasn't at fault /
he tends to go slower than he did before / especially
with his kids in the car / so it takes him longer than
usual to pull up outside the gates of Celeste's place
/ the house itself is up a slight slope leading off the
main road but Aidy stops short even though the
gates are open / is close enough where he is / he
thinks / this is not a house that Aidy has ever lived
in / probably / partly at least / bought with some
of the proceeds of their divorce / years ago now /
*Laters, bro* / Osh says to Leo giving him a spud / *Ta,
Dad* / he says to Aidy / patting him from behind on
his chest before hopping out of the car / phone in
hand / *Hopefully see you at E's match* / he adds /
& before Aidy can get out to embrace his son / hug
him / thank him for a really lovely weekend / the
back door of his Qashqai slams shut / & he's shot off
/ gone / pacing it quick towards the bright red front
door in his sporty shorts & shirt / he watches his
son slot his key in the lock & just before he enters

the house / give his father & brother a little wave /
Aidy smiles as he watches his son disappear inside /
checks his mirrors & pulls away / he'll look up nice
places to have lunch in Letterkenny later tonight / as
soon as he's submitted his story

/ / /

as he heads towards Cavangarden the clouds are
slowly drifting in / skies darkening / colours
changing / just Leo left as Aidy sets off to complete
the final leg of three / *What's your week looking
like, son?* / it's been years since he's had any kind of
meaningful conversation with his eldest / just the
two of them about proper things / not just football
or what new series they've been binging on Netflix
/ but about real life / chats about love & money &
mental health & all that stuff / & Aidy knows that
speaking about these things hasn't always come
naturally to him but something has changed this
weekend / the story he's been writing has shifted
something / *Still got some packing to do . . .* / Leo

answers / Aidy feels all itchy & hot at this response
/ this move has crept up on him faster than he would
have liked / it's just a few weeks now until Leo &
his boyfriend move to Belfast & Aidy is unsure
what to say about it / about their relationship /
thinks he might want to be encouraging / supportive
even / but doesn't quite know how / words not
forming / the commentary from the match the only
thing stopping an awkward silence / deep down /
in all truth / Aidy loves his first-born / of course
he does / but is scared / terrified of losing him to
that troubled city / miles away / gay men in his
day were considered kiddy-fiddlers / he knows he
shouldn't worry as much as he does / times have
changed / & are changing still / but his stomach's all
knotted at the thought of his oldest son not being as
physically close to him as he is now / Aidy changes
the subject / tries to buy time he doesn't have /
can't afford / *I've been working on this story . . . /*
he says / filling the void with something / anything
/ suddenly feeling embarrassed at the thought of
sharing more / but better than the awkward silence

/ Leo looks at his dad then with an expression Aidy
can't read / as he keeps his eyes on the road / . . .
*for a competition thing . . .* / he adds / wondering
about the expression on his son's face now / pride?
/ disappointment? / Leo doesn't even react when
United equalise / a 'worldy' judging by the tone of
Peter Drury's screams / & judging by the sea change
in the atmosphere / Aidy knows he hasn't played
this quite right as he pulls up outside the big house
/ already knows Brenda won't be there / she rarely
is / spends most of her time between Spain & the
Sunshine State these days / married some banker
after her short marriage with Aidy way back when
/ often leaves the house turned B&B for Leo / *Take
care of yourself, son* / an olive-branch offering /
Leo looks at his dad / pauses / despite craving one
/ Aidy knows a hug isn't forthcoming so keeps his
eyes facing the front / *You too* / Leo replies as he
sidles out without turning around & shuts the car
door / perhaps he could have done more / offered to
help with the move / could've asked how Ben was
too / should've put something in the diary before he

left / a celebratory drink or a last Donegal dinner at
La Bella Donna / & now he's kicking himself / on
his way home / back through Ballyshannon / Aidy
listens to Gemma Dunleavy / 'Up De Flats' / & lets
the thoughts of his three kids flit & fill his Qashqai
as the track plays again & again / he floats in it /
basks in it / lets it linger till he's back in Belleek / till
he's turning into his drive / pulling up outside his
house / all alone / key in / once inside his cold house
he opens his fridge & opens one of the two cans of
Guinness he has left

/ / /

he feels better than he has all day / hangover more
or less gone / he hunches over his laptop / cracks his
knuckles / checks the word count / he's nearly there
you know? / just needs a thousand more words or
so / slightly less / just needs to bring this story to
some kind of climactic close / this is the final push
/ no time to waste / he's on the home stretch /
stretching out his dodgy knee as he plonks down

into the chair / now he's back in front of the screen
he's generally feeling a little hopeful about his little
story / but sometimes the positive energy slips /
dips / sometimes he has this strange urge to ctrl A
& delete / but he *needs* this / he reminds himself /
these lines could change everything / he sips more
of his tinny / imagines a new life / one where he's
a proper full-time writer / pounding away on his
long-awaited next bestseller in a swanky study with
a shelf of all his books behind him / holiday home
in the south of Spain / enough rooms for each of his
kids / & a Georgian townhouse in St John's Wood
with Freya from Omaze as his wife / sits in cracked-
leather armchairs drinking fancy South African
white wine & reading Zadie Smith novels / French
double doors leading out onto a generous-sized
garden / Thin Lizzy blaring out of a Bang & Olufsen
Bluetooth speaker / the subject of a BBC *Imagine*
episode or interviewed for the new season of Louis
Theroux / Sunday walks along Regent's Canal that
looks like pea soup without the hock ham / he *needs*
this / knows he's long in the tooth / *this* needs to

work / he writes more about the mystery of grief
/ like the shock of stubbing a toe / wincing from
the discomfort of a new pair of shoes rubbing up
against your heel / or trying / & failing / to break
your fall after one too many pints on a Friday night
/ but there's no mark when you check / no scratch
/ no bruise / no scar / no graze / & you feel cheated
/ confused / conned / grief being that invisible pain
that has outstayed its welcome / has made itself too
comfortable on *your* patch / won't go away / leaves
you feeling empty like going to bed full-stomach
stuffed & waking up empty-stomach starving / an
all-consuming ache that takes stranglehold / Aidy
pushes on / pushes through / he has to / music
playing / 'Luminous' by Einaudi / it feels good
/ fitting / but wishes it was Gemma Dunleavy /
wishes it was 'Up De Flats' / as he describes the fury
felt by the mother at the world choosing to just
move on without her son / nature not healing / he
writes it all down / with the hope these lines might
do something / take him somewhere / act as a kind
of springboard / he's tired of binge-watching box

sets alone / tired of having no-one's hand to hold
/ no-one's frame to embrace / checks his phone /
unsurprisingly / another message from Kateryna
/ but just the one this time / no picture / no saucy
videos / just words / not many either / just a few
/ *How you doing this evening dearest Aidy? As*
*always, I'm thinking of you x*

*/ / /*

in the weeks & months they've been messaging
/ she's never sent a message that feels genuine
/ confirmation / proof there might actually be
something serious between them / not just feet pics
& bank details / he delays replying straight away
/ smile on his face / Aidy takes a big gulp of his
Guinness & gets back to work / adds more lines to
bring the mother's grief to life / tries to describe
her heart breaking / & how she wishes she could
have held her dead son before he left for the UK /
strong-armed him into staying / stopped him from
boarding that shitty no-good plane / months later /

the grief lingers / loiters like a predator in an unlit
alleyway / she waddles from bed to bathroom &
back again / her breakfast this morning was bedside
antidepressants & a Coke Zero / no spa day / luxury
retreat / fancy Moroccan hammam could fix her
now / massage the kinks out of whatever's left of
her broken soul / he writes it all down / trying to
make every little detail count / the words adding up
/ digit by digit / he's on a roll / adds lines to describe
the feeling of feeling entirely bereft by death / doing
everything he can to bring this grief to life / adds a
bit of him in there too / writes from lived experience
/ mixes the mother's grief of losing her son with
his own grief of not knowing his mum / specifically
of her not wanting to know him / it seems / he sips
his Guinness & suddenly snapshots of the state he
got himself in after work the other week flicker into
his mind / a Friday / & instead of driving home
decided to stroll into Enniskillen / noticed how so
many people walked with a strange gait / injury or
ailment / then / unexpectedly / started welling up
at a busker playing Lewis Capaldi / was compelled

to stop & listen for a bit / & in a uncharacteristic
moment of generosity / dropped a crisp tenner in
his empty Costa cup / tears in his eyes before being
brought back to earth by the shouts of a junkie
calling another junkie *a fucking junkie!* / bellowing
back & forth like banshees / someone had sharpied
**FUCK THATCHER** on the wrought-iron
gate of the children's play park up by the cemetery
/ went via the post office / wanting to send a few
postcards to his family in Australia / waited a while
in the queue / stuck behind a wide-feet fogey for
ages / teenage girls behind / Eimear's age roughly
/ with brown paper bags full of crop tops & trackie
bottoms bought in Erneside / sometimes / when he's
in one of his strange moods / he walks through town
like he's re-enacting his final movements before his
death / hyper-aware of the CCTV cameras watching
him & imagines police detectives poring over the
footage / watching it back in slow-motion to try &
find his murderer / then as it started to rain / Aidy
ducked into Granny Annie's / sat there for hours
nursing a half-pint / flipping his beer mat around &

around in his fingers / mindlessly scrolling through Facebook & people-watching / before making his way down the road to Magee's / atmosphere lively / pulled up a pew on a free stool / the perfect spot to watch it all unfurl around him / was definitely one of the oldest people there / didn't feel like drinking anymore / rarely does these days / instead just took it all in / watching the frolicking of others / saw it all / so-called good girls letting their hair down / girls with 'WAP' as their top song on their Spotify Wrapped secretly Shazam-ing the cheesy pop song that was playing / girls with endless X's in their Instagram handle / the evening sloshing around them / old fellas slumped at the bar but allowed to stay by the thick-necked bouncers / *I'll have a Guinness & a line of Charlie, please* / one fella jokes / different colour t-shirt showing underneath his jumper / before stumbling into the gents & breathing in the thick pissy stench / young lad / eighteen-ish / Carhartt socks & bright blue Crocs / licking the perfume off the neck of the girl he'd been flirting with all night / Aidy watched it all /

the Spanish tourist taking her Guinness before the barman had finished topping it up / Aidy watched it all then & writes about it all now / upon leaving was approached by a man selling balloons to the tune of the *Pink Panther* theme tune / streaks of shredded lettuce strewn across the main street / the only people using ATMs were teenagers wanting to buy gear / desperate to get high to stop feeling low / not one of his better birthdays in all truth / another version of this strange manifestation of loss that he's been feeling lately / well . . . / for the last fifty-odd years / life moving on but the grief remaining / resolutely / moments of joy coming & going / like the woman in England who can smell whether someone has Parkinson's / like Wi-Fi reception underground / the feeling all too fleeting / the grief never shrinking / just tightening / strangling / taking stronghold / & how / without warning / or sufficient training / you're just expected to know how to grow around it / lick it right off your lips / simply dismiss it / but it never gets easier / still hard to take / a pill too big to swallow / he was just

twenty-eight / the footballer / his main character /
no age at all / & half a year on she's still struggling
/ the mother / life around her goes on / that school-
bell buzz / petty school-gate drama / restaurants
hum / sticky-floored nightclubs throb / & Aidy can
understand her pain / feels the same / life goes on
& she's just holding on / he is too / the mother too
scared to look in the mirror / too scared to discover
the bulging bags under her eyes / skin discolouring
/ growing signs of some kind of irritation / if this
works out / if he wins this / he has already made
plans to devote time to turning this short story
into something longer / but he just wants to get
the feeling of always feeling like he doesn't belong
. . . down / he feels close now / can almost see the
finish line / can almost taste it / he has the 'Up De
Flats' lyrics stuck in his head / for years he's felt
like the forgotten man / a real Donegal Danny / but
he's a few lines away now from finishing something
he's *actually* proud of / he's suddenly hungry with
relief writing about grief / too late for a spice bag /
he's hungry & sick of feeling alone / he misses the

stickiness of her soles padding across the kitchen
lino / whose kitchen? / whose soles? / he doesn't
exactly know / just doesn't want to live like this
anymore / lukewarm ready meals / crying at John
Lewis Christmas adverts / feels a bit faint thinking
about the future / & what if he never meets his birth
mum ever again? / what then?

/ / /

he writes more / he's tired now but keen to keep
going / maybe he should have tried email? / he
suddenly thinks / maybe the letter was too old-
school / he just wants to meet her so badly / he's
knackered now / heavy-lidded eyes drooping /
morale dropping / feeling rumble-strip rough /
sad & alone / been run ragged this weekend / Aidy
winces getting up / needs a quick stretch / sits
back down / she will never feel full joy again / the
mother / life goes on / through death / world wars /
pandemics / cost-of-living crises / there will be the
odd line of light coming through from somewhere

now & then / from time to time / something
resembling joy / funny TikToks / memes & stuff
/ but for now life goes on / for her / for Aidy / he
switches it up / starts writing to plane noise / thinks
about his main character / dead / jots down more
lines at speed / life goes on / describes passengers
walking on the bobbly bits of the train platform
just to feel something / life goes on / comfortable-
looking but rather ugly Cornish pasty shoes / life
goes on / he won't rest until this story is a success
/ & when it is he will celebrate with a night out in
London / yes / that's what he'll do / life goes on /
he exhales / section three is steadily taking shape
/ a stream of consciousness about life & death /
delicately depicting the presence of death on all our
doorsteps / Aidy needs a piss / badly / but he's on a
roll here / revelling in this slightly panicky passion-
fuelled energy of his story / the words tumbling out
/ words slurred / disparate lines coming together
to form this rough-edged collage / ideas about life
& love & morality & mortality / flying solo but
not flying blind / relishing in the thrill of it / life

moves on & Aidy writes & writes / he's been at it
for nearly two hours straight / his back aches / his
knee is stiff / it always is / his fist is still sore / has
been all weekend / but he feels good / *this* feels good
/ the momentum suddenly feels cup-final loud / like
hitting that sweet spot when clapping / he's not sure
how he's done it but as he looks at the number at
the bottom left corner of the screen / he can see he's
nearly at five thousand words / he won't have time
to print it off now / skim-read it through / make
corrections & suggestions in pencil / not before
the deadline / but he's so nearly there / barely
any of these words existed on Friday / he reminds
himself / but now look! / just as he's about to type
the last few lines / bring the mother character back
into the fore for the denouement / some kind of
lingering final thought / draw his story to some
kind of satisfactory close / some kind of aching end
/ convert it into a PDF so it looks all posh & profesh
/ his phone / face down / starts flashing around the
edges / someone is ringing

Aidy worries for a minute it's work / his manager
telling him not to bother coming in tomorrow / if
it is about the punch he's sorry / so very sorry /
but's it's an unknown number / strange / & in this
day & age with all them crafty cyber-scammers
& catfishers & cryptocurrency con-artists / AI &
that / he tends to ignore random calls these days
/ especially those who have the cheek to ring at
this time on a Sunday / could this be something
to do with Kateryna? / is he in too deep? / is this
someone after more money? / he should be used
to being swindled by now / the more he stares at
the screen / the random nameless number flashing
bright at the top / the more he's tempted to give
this person what for / he pauses / pauses some
more / then presses / answers / waits for a sound /
any sound / on the other end / before putting the
phone closer to his ear / *Hello* / Aidy speaks first
/ adopting a deeper voice than usual / the most
intimidating voice he can muster / ward off dodgy

wrongdoers by sounding as threatening as he can
/ the line isn't great / reception sketchy / there's
sound coming through but heard in fragments / on
& off / loud then quiet / there & then not there

/ / /

*Is that better?* / the other person at the other end
of the line says / clearer than before / as clear as
can be / *Sorry about that, bloody EE!* / he says
irritably / definitely English / London probably /
he sounds nervous / or tired / or ill / there's little
inflection in his voice / it's all monotone / flat / dead
/ . . . *Erm . . . sorry* / he starts / *I wasn't sure I was
going to get through . . .* / he adds / unsure / *This
is Aidy I'm speaking to, right?* / he asks to Aidy's
growing frustration / *Depends who's asking* / he
replies / sternly / not showing his hand / another
long pause / *I don't really know where to begin to
be honest . . .* / another long sigh at the other end
/ Aidy is struggling to understand what's going
on here / & how this random man from England

knows his name / found his number / could this be some kind of prank? / another case of *let's all pick on Aidy* / always the butt of the joke / he's racking his brain trying to work out who this English man is . . . / *It's Shaun* / he says suddenly / this mystery man at the other end of the line / Shaun who? / Wallace? / Aidy is sure he doesn't know any Shauns / . . . *the son of Gloria, your birth mother* / there's a pause like a front door opening / Aidy's heart's beating so fast it's suddenly hurting / face numb too / through the pain & shock & complete disbelief words tumble out / *Did she receive my letter?* / he feels the weight of his question like he's coming up for air / parking up after a long drive / after this surprise comes silence / fleshy in the throat / heavy in the heart / but something's not right / energy wrong / tone off / *She's . . .* / Shaun starts to say / she's what? / desperate to see me? / on her way to Belleek as we speak? / wants me to be part of the family finally? / *I'm sorry but she's . . .* / she's what / spit it out / come on mate / . . . *dead* / the words stab sharp / stab deep / *But did she read my letter?*

/ Aidy hears himself ask / *Does she know I've been trying to connect?* / *Does she know I exist?* / it's two minutes to nine / Aidy has ten twelve tabs open / maybe more / the TV's on / all the lights too / washing machine / dishwasher / he needs a piss / bladder so full it stings / hangnail of right thumb bleeding bright / the deadline looming / his heart hurts but his fist feels better / the cursor hovers over the 'Submit' button / he hasn't had a chance to read it through / he looks at the number at the bottom left corner / stares at the cursor / blinking / at the end of the day it's all just words anyway / *Hello . . . you still there?* / Shaun asks / Aidy doesn't know what to say / doesn't know what to do / what's supposed to happen here / *Hello . . .* / Shaun tries again / *. . . are you still there?* / Aidy doesn't know how to respond / literally can't get anything out / *. . . err . . .* / he starts / then stops / he can hear a racket in the background / this man's wife & kids squabbling or playing or something / laughter mixed with love / *. . . sorry about all the noise* / Shaun says / *You know . . . I've never flown*

*to Ireland before / he adds / Maybe we better have*
*this conversation in person*